Grabill Missionary

3 6678 0000 ____

W9-CDZ-474

"You want me to babysit?" Mike knew *that* wasn't in his job description.

"This kid was in an accident. I need you to keep him away from his mother until she's stabilized," Dr. Ana Ramírez said.

Mike gulped as Ana walked away. Saying no wasn't an option. He was going to look after the little boy even though he knew nothing about children.

The boy gripped the gurney that held his mother. The sight of the child broke Mike's heart.

"The doctors need to take care of your mom, buddy," Mike explained calmly. "Will you come with me?" When the boy nodded, Mike put him in bed in another room.

"Will you stay with me?" the kid whispered.

"As long as I can." Mike took the child's hand. For the first time since he'd started work at the hospital, he felt like he belonged here.

Books by Jane Myers Perrine

Love Inspired

The Path to Love #310
Love's Healing Touch #414

JANE MYERS PERRINE

grew up in Kansas City, Missouri, has a B.A. from Kansas State University and has an M.Ed. in Spanish from the University of Louisville. She has taught high school Spanish in five states and now she teaches in the beautiful hill country of Texas. Her husband is minister of a Christian church in Central Texas where Jane teaches an adult Sunday school class.

Jane was a finalist in the Regency category for a Golden Heart Award. Her short pieces have appeared in the *Houston Chronicle, Woman's World* and other publications. The Perrines share their home with two spoiled cats and an arthritic cocker spaniel. Readers can visit her Web site www.janemyersperrine.com.

Love's Healing Touch
Jane Myers Perrine

Steeple
Hill®

Published by Steeple Hill Books™

If you purchased this book without a cover you should be aware that this book is stolen property. It was reported as "unsold and destroyed" to the publisher, and neither the author nor the publisher has received any payment for this "stripped book."

STEEPLE HILL BOOKS

Steeple
Hill®

ISBN-13: 978-0-373-81328-5
ISBN-10:   0-373-81328-7

LOVE'S HEALING TOUCH

Copyright © 2007 by Jane Myers Perrine

All rights reserved. Except for use in any review, the reproduction or utilization of this work in whole or in part in any form by any electronic, mechanical or other means, now known or hereafter invented, including xerography, photocopying and recording, or in any information storage or retrieval system, is forbidden without the written permission of the editorial office, Steeple Hill Books, 233 Broadway, New York, NY 10279 U.S.A.

This is a work of fiction. Names, characters, places and incidents are either the product of the author's imagination or are used fictitiously, and any resemblance to actual persons, living or dead, business establishments, events or locales is entirely coincidental.

This edition published by arrangement with Steeple Hill Books.

® and TM are trademarks of Steeple Hill Books, used under license. Trademarks indicated with ® are registered in the United States Patent and Trademark Office, the Canadian Trade Marks Office and in other countries.

www.SteepleHill.com

Printed in U.S.A.

Come to me, all you that are weary and are carrying heavy burdens, and I will give you rest. Take my yoke upon you, and learn from me; for I am gentle and humble in heart, and you will find rest for your souls. For my yoke is easy, and my burden is light.

—*Matthew* 11:28-30

This book is dedicated to my family:

My parents, "Dr. Bob" and Martha Myers,
who took me to church, to Sunday school,
to youth group, to choir, to camp…

My big brother, Mike Myers, and my sister,
Patricia Myers Norton, who were such wonderful
Christian examples as I was growing up and are
wonderful friends now. Thank you.

And, as always, to my husband, George,
for his love and support—and for forty-one years
of inspirational sermons. I only slept
through a few, honey.

Chapter One

"Coming through," a nurse shouted as she pushed a crash cart down the hall of the emergency room.

Mike Fuller leaped away and landed in the path of a gurney being moved at breakneck speed. "Hey, you," shouted the orderly as he swerved around Mike, "grab the door to the elevator and keep it open."

Mike dashed toward the closing door and held it open until the orderly and his patient arrived. After the doors shut behind them, Mike again entered the E.R. and navigated through a hallway so crowded with patients on gurneys that there was only a narrow pathway between them. Ahead was the central desk where he'd been told to check in with the nursing staff.

No one was there.

A glance through the window on his right showed a waiting room filled with people. From outside the building, the siren of an approaching ambulance wailed, a sound which warred with the sounds inside the building—shouts of medical personnel and the bellow of the loudspeaker calling doctors and spewing forth codes. Amid the noise, medical staff hurried past, stopping in one cubicle or another.

Mike inhaled the stifling scent of disinfectant and looked around him. Even if he was only an orderly—well, *clinical assistant,* but everyone knew that meant *orderly*—he was here, in Austin University Hospital during the late shift. The commotion made him feel alive and want to be part of it. Unfortunately, he had no idea what he should do. Whether he was an orderly or a CA, he could do only what he was told. That had been pounded into him during his training and three-day orientation.

"Orderly."

He turned to see a beautiful woman watching him. She was short, but beneath her open lab coat—which meant she was a doctor so he shouldn't be noticing how attractive she was— were curves, delightful curves. Right now, he had too much going on in his life to even look at a woman, but only a dead man wouldn't check out this one. She was exactly the kind of woman he'd always liked in the past—except for that one mistake with tall, blond Cynthia.

This doctor's dark hair was pulled back in a round little knot. She had beautiful golden-brown skin and brown eyes, which, he realized, were glaring at him. In addition, her lovely pink lips were forming words. "I need you," she said as she pointed at him, "to check the vitals of the patients in the hall. Then get gloves and a bucket and start cleaning Exam 6."

"But—" Mike started.

"I know, that's housekeeping's job but with the mess tonight, we're all going to have to pitch in on everything." Then she walked away, saying, "Thank you," over her shoulder as she entered one of the cubicles.

"I see you've met Dr. Ramírez, the head resident in the E.R.," said a nurse as she returned to her desk. "She can be demanding at times, but she's a great doctor." She glanced at Mike's name tag. "Welcome, Fuller. I'm Pat. We can really use you tonight."

"Is it always this busy?"

"Depends. Tonight there was a chemical spill south of town." She picked up a marker and started writing names on the dry-erase board. "We've got injuries from three traffic accidents and a gunshot wound in Trauma 1. And a family in a house fire." She shook her head. "A lot of other injuries I can't remember. A fairly normal night here."

Then she sat. "Might as well get you started. I'll have Williams show you around." Her gaze scanned the area. "Williams, come on over here."

When the brawny orderly arrived, he smiled to expose a gold front tooth. "Glad to see you, man. We're two orderlies short so I'm working too hard."

"Mike Fuller." He held out his hand.

"No time for that." Williams slapped Mike on the back. "Come with me."

"Dr. Ramírez wanted me to—"

"Check the vitals on the patients in the hall. Let's get going." The other orderly handed Mike a stethoscope. "You'll be supervised by the head nurse, but everyone in this place will give you orders. Just do anything anyone tells you to do, and you'll be fine."

The rest of the shift was spent in hard work, eight solid hours with only a few minutes break here and there.

Once he found himself whispering, "Dear Lord, please get me through this." The prayer surprised him because, right now, he and God weren't on the best of terms.

Once, as he pushed a gurney toward the elevator, he passed Dr. Ramírez making notes in a chart at the nurses' station.

"Look but don't touch," Williams warned him. "Yes, she's pretty but she's a doctor. She makes sure we all know that. Her body language says, 'Keep away.'"

Mike didn't read it that way exactly, but staying away from Dr. Ramírez was good advice, both personally and professionally.

After the first wave of those who'd been affected by the chemical spill had been taken care of, two ambulances arrived from a gang shooting. The vitals of the first kid to come in had dropped and the EMTs couldn't get the wounds to stop bleeding.

While everyone hovered around the gangbanger, Dr. Ramírez looked at a tiny Hispanic woman on another gurney who'd been an unlucky bystander, the EMT had said.

The doctor picked up the paramedic's notes and read them. Finished, she said, "I want that woman in there." She pointed at Mike then at Trauma 2.

He nodded, grabbed the gurney and pushed it into the cubicle Dr. Ramírez had indicated. On the count of three, he and a nurse's aide named Gracie moved the woman to the trauma bed. Gracie cut and peeled off the woman's blood-soaked clothing, then put her in a gown. The patient closed her eyes, whimpered a little and bit her lower lip.

"Get a drip started," Dr. Ramírez told a nurse. Then, her voice soft and low, she said to the patient, "*¿Le duele mucho, Señora Sánchez?*"

Mike remembered enough of his college Spanish to know that she'd asked the elderly woman if she hurt. The patient nodded.

The doctor pulled the blanket and gown down to study the area on the patient's right shoulder the paramedics had treated. "*¿Aquí?*" She gently pressed on the area around the wound which had begun to seep blood.

"*Ay, me duele mucho.*"

He could tell from her expression that the pressure had hurt the woman, a lot.

"Help me turn her on the left side," Dr. Ramírez said to Mike. "Slowly and carefully." Once Mrs. Sánchez was turned, Dr. Ramírez ran her hand over the patient's shoulder and back. "No exit wound," she said.

"Okay." Dr. Ramírez glanced up at Mike. "After the IV is going, take her to the OR. I'll call the surgeon."

Before Mike could transfer Mrs. Sánchez to a

gurney, the doctor took Mrs. Sánchez's hand and said, *"Señora, todo va a estar bien. Cálmese. El cirujano es buena gente."*

Something about everything being okay, to calm down because the surgeon was a good guy, Mike translated for himself. The elderly woman took a deep breath and unclenched her fists as Mike rolled the gurney away.

Seemed Dr. Ramírez was more than a tough professional. She cared for her patients, understood what they needed. That was the kind of doctor he wanted to be, the kind he would be if he could get the money together to go back to med school.

Because he'd been in foster care, the state had paid college and medical school tuition. During four years of college and one of medical school, he'd roomed with four guys in a cheap apartment and worked part-time to make it through. But with the extra money he needed to rent the house, buy food and cover whatever expenses came up until his mother and little brother could get on their feet, he had to work full-time. No way he could go to medical school and support them, which he had to do. After his father had deserted them almost twenty years earlier, Mike was pretty much the head of the family.

He'd considered other options but couldn't

afford the time off and the seven-hundred-dollar fee for paramedic training. With overtime, he'd make more as an orderly than teaching high school, plus he'd be in a hospital. All that made the decision to be an orderly easy.

By seven the next morning, he was so worn-out he moved in a fog. This was hard work, but he loved the feel of the hospital, the certainty that amid the commotion, all the patients would be helped, that he was doing good, meaningful, healing work.

The sight of Dr. Ramírez added a lot to that positive feeling. After all, he could appreciate the view, if only from a distance. At this moment and maybe for several years, with the mess that was his life, all he could enjoy was the view.

A week after his first day in the E.R., the phone rang in the small house Mike rented. When he answered, his younger brother, Tim, said in a shaky voice, "I had an accident, but it wasn't my fault."

Mike held the telephone tightly. "Are you all right?"

Tim cleared his throat and spoke without the quiver. "Yeah, I'm fine. It was minor."

Knowing Tim, a minor accident meant the car still had most of the tires and not *all* the glass was broken. "And you're really okay?"

"The paramedics checked me over. No problems."

"Where are you? How will you get home?"

"The cops'll bring me. Talk to you then." Tim hung up.

Mike disconnected the phone, put it on the end table, and dropped onto the sofa. He was glad Tim was okay. Mike whispered a quick, "Thank you, God, for taking care of Tim."

Sometimes Mike wondered if God ever got anything done while watching over Tim.

Even with a minor accident, the insurance company would total the car which meant he wouldn't get enough money to buy another anytime soon.

Mike hadn't been in a fix like this since he was eighteen. Of course, this time he wouldn't take a gun and hold up a convenience store, which showed he had learned something over the past six years. And this time most of the problems weren't his. He'd inherited them from other people.

Thank goodness the wreck hadn't happened last week when he'd moved from his apartment to this rental house. Now, for the first time in eight years, he'd be living with his family: his eighteen-year-old brother, who'd just been released from the state foster care system, and their mother, who was getting out of prison where she'd served time for fraud. He wouldn't want the living arrangements any other way, but it was still a big change.

He leaned back and put his feet up on a cardboard box marked Kitchen. He was supposed to take his cousin Francie to the doctor in an hour and the hospital had called and asked him to come in early for his shift. In a few days, he had to meet his mother's bus and get her settled in the house.

But he had no car.

No, he hadn't caused most of these problems, but he couldn't shift them to his much-loved but equally scatterbrained mother or his absent-minded and immature younger brother.

He couldn't lean on Francie. She had enough to deal with, what with the baby coming, fixing up her house and finding time to be with her husband. Besides, he owed her big-time. She'd put her life on hold for him, taken the rap for him when he'd been young and almost irredeemably stupid.

No, he couldn't toss this on Francie, which left *him* in charge. Not a prospect that filled him with joy.

When the phone rang again, he picked it up and hoped it wasn't more bad news. "Hey."

"How's it going?" Francie asked.

"Tim wrecked my car."

"How is he?"

"He says he's fine, but I can't take you to the doctor's office. No car."

"I'll pick you up. After you bring me home, you can use my car as long as you need it."

"Francie, should you be driving? Didn't you say your doctor had some concerns?"

"The doctor hasn't told me to stop driving. Besides, if you have my car, I can't drive."

"But…"

Ignoring the interruption, Francie said, "You have to have a car. Brandon will agree with me. If it makes you feel better, you can be my chauffeur, take me anywhere I want to go," she said in her don't-argue voice. "See you in twenty minutes."

After Mike hung up the phone, he went to the window to watch for the cop car bringing Tim home.

When the police arrived, he moved to the front door and held it open for Tim. "Let me look at you," Mike said as his brother sauntered inside, bravado showing in his swagger.

"This time it wasn't my fault." When Tim stumbled a little and put his hand on the wall to steady himself, he lost a lot of his macho attitude. "It really wasn't, Mike."

Tim was tall with dark hair pulled back in a ponytail. Two years of lifting weights had put some muscle on him. Now he had wide shoulders with an even wider chip perched there.

As he scrutinized Tim, Mike saw several facial lacerations and a couple of bruises beginning to form. "Let me check you out."

"The paramedics cleared me. Why do you have to, Mike? You're not a doctor."

Mike drew in a breath at the painful reminder that no, he wasn't a doctor and wasn't likely to be one. "Just go along with me. Let me practice on you."

Tim shrugged then winced at the pain the movement brought. "Well, okay. If it makes you happy." With a grimace, he pulled the T-shirt over his head.

"How did it happen?" Mike ran his fingers down Tim's ribs, feeling for any knots or abnormalities and watching his brother's reaction.

"I was driving along Guadalupe and this other car didn't even slow down, ran right into the front of your car. The police said it was the other guy's fault. Ouch. What are you doing?"

"Almost through." Mike's hands brushed over a discolored diagonal line across Tim's chest. "Glad you were wearing your seat belt."

"For once." Tim nodded. "Guess I must have been listening to you."

"Also, for once." Mike looked into Tim's eyes. "You look okay, but you're going to be sore. Put some ice on your face."

"Yeah, sure." He limped off.

Mike shook his head and hoped Tim would grow up before he did any real damage to himself or someone else.

"Thanks for loaning me your car." Mike backed Francie's little red Focus out of the drive and turned south. He glanced at his cousin, taking warmth from her smile. Dark curls surrounded her face, a little fuller now in pregnancy.

As he stopped at a light, he noticed the worried frown on her face. "So how's little Ebenezer doing?"

"I wish you wouldn't call the baby that." She laughed, the lovely, happy sound that always made Mike feel great. "A girl named Ebenezer? It would be terrible enough for a boy." She paused before adding in a worried voice, "As I said, I'm having a few physical problems. I'm pretty sure the doctor will tell me to cut down my activities until I deliver."

"What's going on?"

"Unless you're the father or the grandparents of this baby, you don't want to know." Her voice trembled a little.

"Francie, I took a course in genetics, embryology and reproduction my first and only year of medical school."

"Well, then I'd prefer not to tell you. It's kind of personal." She softened the words with a smile.

"Anyway, that's why Brandon wanted you to drive me since he couldn't get off today. We're not sure what the doctor's going to say." Tears shimmered in her eyes. "We first-time parents worry a lot."

He signaled and turned on the ramp to Loop 1 or the MoPac as everyone in Travis County called the highway. "Take care of yourself, okay?"

"I do. And I will." She sighed. "So you might as well drive the car. Brandon or his family will drive me anywhere so I won't need it. If using my car makes you feel guilty, bring me some of Manny's good soup from the diner every week or two."

"Fine with me." He stopped at a light and turned toward her. "Mom's coming home next week. I'll be able to pick her up at the bus station."

"Are you excited to see her after—how long has it been? Seven, eight years?"

"Eight." He considered the question. "Hard to say. I'm excited *and* worried both. The three of us haven't lived together since she left. We'll be crowded in that tiny house." He stepped on the gas as the light changed. "Tim and I have to share the second bedroom. The owner has bunk beds in there." Mike grimaced. "Fortunately, Tim's still enough of a kid to like sleeping in the top bunk."

"Oh, and you're such an old man you couldn't get up there?"

"I don't want to get up there." He turned off on

the Thirty-fourth Street exit and drove a block before he said, "There's another reason I'm worried." His hands beat out a rhythm on the steering wheel. "You know how much I love her, but how's Mom going to move on from prison life? She's never worked. What if she wants to forge paintings again?"

"That's hard, Mike." She shook her head. "I don't know. Guess you'll have to lay down the law, which is *not* something this family is good about accepting. I'll pray for you. You might do some praying for yourself."

He nodded. No use telling the woman who'd introduced him to church and helped him develop his faith that prayer had become only habit. It didn't work for him anymore.

Francie folded her hands over the roundness of her stomach and struggled to find a comfortable position. "How's Cynthia?"

"Don't know. Haven't seen her for a while." He signaled for a turn, carefully kept his gaze on the road and refused to meet her eyes. "Not a lot of traffic. We should get to the doctor's office in plenty of time."

"Don't change the subject." She pushed herself around in the seat to look at him. "What happened with Cynthia? I thought you two were made for each other."

"I thought so, too." He clenched his jaw, not wanting to say more, but he knew Francie wouldn't leave him alone until he explained. "When I told her I had to quit medical school to work, that we couldn't get married for two or three years, not until Mom and Tim are on their own, she said she wouldn't wait."

"Oh, I'm sorry."

"She wants to marry a doctor, not an orderly who lives with his mother and brother." Her departure had filled him with an emptiness it would take time to fill, so at least he wouldn't hurt every time he thought about her. "I don't blame her."

"You should blame her. She's a shallow ninny."

He didn't feel like it, but he had to laugh.

"Why aren't you angry? You should be furious," she said.

"I thought Christians didn't get angry."

"Well, in some situations, like when your former fiancée is being a shallow ninny, I think it's okay. For a while."

Well, then, yes, he'd been angry when he realized Cynthia hadn't wanted *him.* How could he have misjudged her feelings and character? How could she have fooled him so completely? Maybe he was the idiot for believing she loved him. It would be a long time before he opened himself to that kind of hurt again.

"When did this happen?" she asked.

"About a month ago. When I made the decision for Mom to live with me instead of going to a halfway house, I told Cynthia."

"Well, I'm put out with her. I'd like to talk to that girl, set her straight about what's important in life."

"There's nothing you can do." He shook his head. "But Brandon and little Ebenezer are blessed to have you watching over them."

"I'm the one who's blessed. I have a wonderful husband whose family loves me and this baby coming. I have you and Tim and Aunt Tessie will be home soon. What more could I want?"

Ana Dolores Ramírez—Ana Dolores Ramírez, *M.D.*—tossed a newspaper off the only comfortable chair in the gray, dingy break room and fell into it. After taking a drink of her cold coffee, she leaned back, almost asleep.

What an evening: a terrible accident on I-35, and a fire in a crowded restaurant, all that in addition to the normal everyday emergencies like broken bones, ODs and injuries from gang and domestic violence. Why had she ever thought she wanted to work in an emergency room?

Well, yes, she knew. She loved the excitement, the challenge, the urgency to save people, the fight against death, bringing healing from tumult and despair.

Another reason was the memory of the doctors who had worked so hard to save her leg and the staff in the E.R. who had saved her mother's life.

"It's harder than it looks, isn't it?" Dr. Leslie Harmon, the Director of Emergency Services, entered the lounge.

Ana yawned. "Why are you here so late?"

"I was called in when the cases started to back up. I wanted to come in during a busy stretch on this shift to evaluate how the E.R. staff handles a heavy load."

"How'd we do?"

"Very well." Dr. Harmon rubbed her neck and rotated her shoulders. "I was particularly impressed with one of the CAs. The new guy— dark-haired, handsome kid—seemed really sharp. Who is he?"

Before she could reply, Ana's pager went off. Checking the message, she pulled herself up with a groan. "Not a very long break, but I've got to go." She gulped the last of her coffee and tossed the paper cup in the overflowing trash can as she headed back to the emergency room.

"What's coming in?" Ana pushed through the swinging doors, instantly alert. Paramedics pushed gurneys into the hallway while a clerk wrote the names of the incoming patients on the large white board at the central desk and nurses began to take vitals. Instant activity and a huge increase in the noise level.

"Another traffic accident," the new orderly said.

What *was* his name? She took a peek at his ID tag as she picked up a chart to make notes in. "Thanks, Fuller." As Dr. Harmon had said, he seemed pretty bright. More than just a strong body to lift and position patients. Earlier tonight, he'd recognized the signs of shock and taken quick action, more like a paramedic. He'd also helped with triage, stepping in when he saw how thin the staff was stretched. His assessments hadn't been perfect, but he'd done well enough with those minor cases. After she'd quickly doubled-checked his decisions, she'd been able to concentrate on major traumas.

As the injured were quickly evaluated and moved to treatment rooms, to surgery or to wait in the hall, Ana noticed a boy about six years old standing by one of the gurneys. The woman on the gurney was pale, her eyes closed. Blood stained the bandages the EMTs had applied to her forehead and chest.

When his mother's gurney was pulled into a cubicle, the boy grabbed the side of it and ran to keep up. "Mama," he sobbed.

"Fuller," Ana called.

After he pushed a gurney against the wall, Mike hurried over to where Dr. Ramírez stood next a gurney with a little boy hanging on to it.

"This kid came in with a family from an accident. Please take care of him."

"What? Babysit?" He didn't remember that on the job description. His duties were all medical and nursing.

"We need to keep him away from his mother until we can stabilize her. Find the paramedics. Ask them if he has family here or if there's someone coming to pick him."

"Shouldn't social services—"

"Yes, they should and they usually do take care of the children of our patients, but they're backed up and shorthanded. Can't be here for a couple of hours. I need to treat his mother now. I'd appreciate your handling this."

While Mike watched and wondered what he

should do next, she bent her knees to be on the child's level. "My name's Ana. What's your name?"

The child studied her solemnly. "Stevie."

"Well, Stevie, because your mommy was in an accident, we need to patch her up a little. I promise we'll take very good care of her." Gesturing toward Mike, she added, "This young man is going to keep you company while we do that. Okay?"

Then she stood and turned back toward the trauma room.

What was he going to do? Mike gulped as he watched her walk away. Saying "no" wasn't an option. "But, Dr. Ramírez, I don't know anything about children," he protested.

"Do it," she said in the clear, firm voice Mike figured no one ignored. "Please."

He turned and started toward the boy as Dr. Ramírez entered a cubicle.

No one, not even lowly orderlies, ignored Dr. Ramírez's voice when it got that certain tone. For that reason, yes, he was going to look after the boy even though, no, he didn't know anything about children.

The boy slumped, his spine curved in exhaustion, but still he kept a tight hold on the gurney that held his mother.

The sight of the child broke Mike's heart. Even worse, he had no idea of what to do. Mike squatted so he was on the same level as the boy's sad eyes. "Hi, Stevie. Where's your family?"

The child shook with sobs and clung more tightly to the gurney.

That had gone really well. Trying again, Mike took the child's hand from the rail and held it although the boy fought to put it back. Was this the right thing to do?

"The doctors need to take care of your mother, buddy," Mike explained calmly. "They can't get around very well with you here."

The child looked at his hand in Mike's then glanced up. "Is she going to be okay?"

"These are the best doctors in the world. They're going to do everything they can to make sure she's all right, but they need enough room to do that."

The boy nodded and stopped his efforts to pull his hand from Mike's.

Mike wiped the child's eyes and nose as he stuffed a handful of tissues in the kid's free hand. "Well, Stevie, do you want to thank the paramedics who helped you? They're really cool guys." When the boy didn't resist, Mike led him into the hall.

"The paramedics are down there." When Mike pointed the boy nodded. "I'm going to talk to them now."

Yawning, Stevie pulled away to wiggle onto a chair. He leaned back and closed his eyes as Mike walked toward the emergency cntrance. The flashing red lights of ambulances pulling up outside lit up the area in flickering streaks of red.

"Hey, guys," Mike greeted the paramedics, keeping his voice low. "Did you bring that kid in?" He gestured toward Stevie.

"Yeah, an accident on MLK. The family in a van was hit when a drunk ran a light."

"What are the kid's injuries?"

"Didn't find anything serious. Probably should have that cut on his forehead checked later, but that's it."

"Do you have a last name? Any identification? Is there family around?"

"The family members who came in with him are all in the E.R., pretty badly injured. The cops are running the name down and getting in touch with relatives," the older paramedic said.

"Thanks."

As he walked back down the corridor, he saw Stevie had fallen asleep. Mike picked him up and carried him to the E.R.

"Orderly," Dr. Yamaguchi, the on-call orthopedic surgeon, said as Mike entered the department. "Now."

Mike nodded at Stevie. "Dr. Ramírez wants me to take care of this kid. His mother's in the E.R. and we can't find a family member."

Dr. Yamaguchi glanced at the kid. "Put him in the emergency bed on the end and check on him when you can, but you have to transport patients."

"Yes, sir."

For the next few hours, Mike checked on Stevie whenever he wasn't pushing gurneys or following the instructions from the medical staff.

Once when Mike entered the cubicle where Stevie had been sleeping, Dr. Ramírez was trying to examine him. Stevie had pulled away from her and cowered as far away from the doctor as possible.

"Hey, buddy, it's okay. Remember those great doctors I told you about?" Mike asked. Stevie nodded. "This is one of them."

"Will you stay?" the kid whispered.

"As long as I can." Mike took Stevie's hand.

"Guess you're here for a while," Dr. Ramírez said.

"Guess so." The prospect would have alarmed Mike a few hours ago but not now. For the first time since he started work, he felt as if he belonged here, as if he had an important role to play and this was part of it.

"Orderly," came a shout from another exam room. "Transport to X-ray."

Then again, maybe not.

Chapter Two

"Good job, Fuller." Dr. Ramírez's voice echoed through the now-empty hall in front of the curtained cubicles of the E.R.

Her voice wasn't exactly friendly, but she didn't sound as if she were ready to chew him out.

"I appreciate the way you pitched in tonight, picking up wherever you were needed." She pulled off her latex gloves, tossed them in the hazardous-waste bin and said, "Thanks for taking care of the boy until his uncle showed up."

Then she smiled at him. Not a big smile. Just a slight turning up of her lips. Still, it was a great look compared to her usual serious expression. Now her eyes sparkled a bit and a dimple appeared on her cheek. For an instant, she assumed the appearance of a human being, a real person, not a doctor.

Probably noticing his confused look, she allowed her usual professional expression to slide across her features again. Then she said in a voice a bit softer than her usual this-is-what-you-have-to-do tone, "Fuller, let me buy you a cup of coffee. There's something I want to discuss with you. Purely professional. Nothing personal."

He wondered what *purely professional* meant and why she had given him that smile. Probably didn't mean a thing to her but it was the first almost-full smile he'd ever seen from her. It was a dazzler.

If he wanted to keep things professional, he shouldn't join Dr. Ramírez for coffee. Meeting Dr. Ramírez outside the E.R. seemed odd to him, but he deserved a little bit of the good stuff—and Dr. Ramírez was really good stuff.

"Yes, ma'am, um, Doctor…Ramírez." He hadn't babbled like that since he'd asked Maribel Suárez out when he was a shrimp in the tenth grade. He cleared his throat and said, "I have to restock a room. Meet you in the cafeteria."

When she left, he checked cabinets in Exam 1, made sure equipment had been replaced in the correct cabinets, and replaced gauze, tape and other supplies that were low. As he worked, he replayed the incident with Dr. Ramírez and felt like an idiot. Since Cynthia broke up with him, he'd been questioning everything in his life, but there was nothing unusual here. The idea she might put a move on him in the middle of a hospital cafeteria was crazy…but very appealing.

He almost slapped himself for that last thought.

Finished, he stripped off his gloves, washed his hands and splashed water on his face. Then he ran damp fingers through his hair as he attempted to make out his reflection in the paper towel holder.

"Hot date, Fuller?" the tall, balding RN asked him as he came through the curtains. What was his name? Oh, yeah, Sam Mitchelson. "Couldn't help but hear the invitation from back there."

"Just a cup of coffee. Like she said, 'Nothing personal.'" Mike tossed the towel away and moved toward the door.

"That's more than any of us, including doctors, have been asked to share. You must possess something special to rate that."

Mike grinned. "Only good looks, high intelligence and great charm."

"Don't forget she's a doctor, Fuller," he said to Mike's back. "If you want to keep your job, never disagree with a doctor."

Mike left the E.R. and headed toward the cafeteria, passing a row of wheelchairs outside X-ray and dodging a crowd getting off the elevator as he walked down the main corridor.

Macho posturing aside, Mike reminded himself again she'd asked him for coffee, only coffee, not a date. As he'd told himself a million times, he had no interest in a relationship and no time, but his response showed he found Dr. Ramírez very attractive. His reaction to her had him thinking that Cynthia hadn't completely killed his interest in women.

Just past the hallway to ICU, he turned to open the door to the cafeteria. The usual mix of medical personnel and family members of patients sat at the square tables. Straight ahead by the windows was Dr. Ramírez with another doctor.

Maybe this wasn't a good idea.

From her table, Ana watched Fuller enter the cafeteria. Tall and handsome with broad shoulders, he looked great in scrubs. That was pure observation, not attraction, she told herself. His height and those broad shoulders made it easier for him to move and transport patients.

When he saw her, he paused and looked a little uncertain. His confusion was probably because Dr. Craddock, the chief of staff, sat next to her, flirting with her. At least thirty years older than she and married, the fool was flirting.

The closer the orderly got to the table, the more obvious Craddock's attention became. Thank goodness they would soon be interrupted.

Fuller stopped when he saw Craddock still talking. He backed away, but she beckoned him forward with a wave.

As he reached the table, Fuller said, "Hello, Dr. Craddock." At her gesture, he dropped into the chair next to Craddock. She pushed a cup of coffee closer to Fuller.

"Hello." Dr. Craddock studied the orderly with one eyebrow raised. "And you are?"

"Mike Fuller. I'm a CA in the E.R." He poured cream in his coffee and stirred it.

"Oh? An orderly?" Craddock's voice and that still-raised brow left no doubt he felt the orderly shouldn't be sitting with two doctors.

"I asked Mr. Fuller to join me. I need to discuss something with him." She smiled at Craddock and gave his hand a sisterly pat. That should put him in his place.

Craddock stood. "I see that I'm the one who's not needed here."

"Dr. Craddock doesn't approve of your ignoring

the hospital social order." Fuller watched the older man move away to join a table of doctors.

"Doctors can be a rigid bunch." She picked up her coffee and took a sip. "But that's not what I wanted to talk to you about." She rubbed her thumb along the side of the cup before she looked up at him. "Fuller, I've watched how you handle situations. You're intelligent and capable."

"Thank you."

He must wonder where this conversation was going. Had she thoughtlessly put him in an awkward situation? Probably so. That's what she got for pushing herself into other people's lives. They weren't always grateful.

"You're an excellent clinical assistant."

He nodded.

"You must have a high-school diploma or a GED or you wouldn't be working here."

He nodded again and gazed over her shoulder toward something behind her.

"Do you have any college hours?"

He scrutinized her face for a moment. "I'm not comfortable with this conversation, Dr. Ramírez. Is there a reason for your questions?" he said, politely but clearly setting boundaries.

"Yes, there is, and, honestly, I want to encourage you."

He took a gulp of coffee.

"Do you have any college hours?" The question sounded rude. She really needed to work on her delivery.

He paused before nodding, again not meeting her eyes.

She was stymied. He clearly wasn't going to give her any more information than he had to, and he didn't have to give her any. "I know I have no right to ask you, but I'd really appreciate it if you'd answer a question or two." After a pause when the orderly didn't say a word, she added, "Please."

When he raised an eyebrow but didn't say no, she asked, "How many college hours?"

"I have a degree." He drank the rest of his coffee, placed the cup on the table and pushed the chair back.

"Please don't go." She put her hand on his.

The touch was *not* the friendly pat she'd intended. As she pulled her hand away, she glanced up to gauge his reaction. His eyes held a spark of interest before he looked down at his empty cup. The man had gorgeous brown eyes, a slight stubble on his cheeks and a square chin. A pleasant glow spread through her. Obviously, more was involved in her feelings for Fuller than mentor for student. Why hadn't she noticed that before she asked him to meet her for coffee?

"Dr. Ramírez, I prefer not to continue this discussion." His words were polite but, when he stood, he glared at her, as much of a glare as an orderly dared give a doctor. She couldn't blame him.

"I'm sorry, Fuller. I don't mean to make you feel uneasy." She forced her attitude back to the purely professional. "I don't have a gift for subtlety, and I know I don't have the right to expect you to sit down and talk to me, but I'd really be grateful if you would."

At least he didn't bolt for the door. Instead, he pulled his chair back to the table, sat and asked in a voice that showed more than a little exasperation, "Why?"

"Fuller, I'm impressed with you."

She tapped on her cup. When she looked into his eyes, he immediately lowered them. "You are intelligent and have so much ability. I'd like to encourage you to go back to school, to pursue a career in medicine or science."

"Thank you." He fiddled with the handle of the cup.

A lot of playing with their cups, Ana noted. Obviously neither of them felt comfortable with the exchange.

"Have you thought about being a doctor?" she asked bluntly in an effort to hurry the conversation along.

"Tried med school. One year. Didn't work out."

"It didn't work out?" she repeated.

Ignoring her question, he said, "Thank you for the coffee, Dr. Ramírez," placing great emphasis on *doctor*.

"You're welcome."

This time he did bolt for the door.

The conversation had not gone the way she'd planned it. She'd acted pushy and nosy. She'd sounded like a superior expecting the orderly to comply with whatever she demanded.

Obviously he had no desire to discuss this or anything with her. Why should he? He seemed like a very private person, just like her father.

No matter. She wasn't about to give up on Fuller. He should be a doctor or a nurse or a medical technician, not an orderly, and she was going to help him see that.

As *her* mother had said, Ana always had to have a project. Fuller seemed to be her latest one.

She'd find out what he meant by, "Didn't work out," another time.

Mike strode back to the E.R. to finish his shift. What right did the woman have to interrogate him? To expect him to sit there while she dug for personal information? Why hadn't he left earlier?

He threw a swinging door open with one hand and watched it hit the wall with a satisfying smack. But when he got to the E.R., an RN shouted, "Fuller, transfer."

He didn't have time to think about Dr. Ramírez's prying now. Maybe he should remember the other parts, the good parts: he'd had coffee with a beautiful woman and all the male staff was jealous. In addition, Dr. Ramírez had complimented him on his intelligence and how well he was doing. After the recent problems in his life, it made him feel a lot better.

Only two hours later, Mike was asleep at home when the phone rang. He pulled himself out of bed and dragged his tired body into the living room. Light filtered through curtains, which made it possible for him to find the phone on the coffee table but not before he narrowly avoided falling over a box of clothes.

"Good morning," Francie said. "Will you please drive me to church this morning? Wake your brother up and bring him, too."

Mike glanced at his watch through eyes still blurry with sleep. He groaned. "I've only been asleep for an hour. Why don't you let me sleep a few more?"

"Because church will be over by then. You can take a long nap when you get home. Or you can sleep through the sermon."

"Reverend Miller won't like that."

"But God will be glad you're there. Besides, you said you'd take me wherever I need to go."

"Aren't you supposed to be taking it easy?"

"The doctor said church is fine as long as I don't drive."

"What about Brandon?" Could he think of any more reasons to go back to bed? If this one didn't work, he'd have to go, because he could never tell Francie no.

"He's at a training session in Dallas," she explained patiently. "Well?"

"Okay, I'll pick you up at ten."

"Thanks. Bring Tim."

Driving her to church was the least he could do. When he was eighteen, he'd held up a convenience store. He groaned, hating to relive that act and its consequences. To save him, so he could be a doctor, Francie had confessed and was serving time before he could take the blame himself. They were the same height and he'd worn a ski mask and jacket so she looked like the person in the surveillance tape.

He'd made a terrible, stupid mistake, and she'd paid for it. He still struggled to figure out why he'd done it—heredity, Francie would say—and to make it up to her somehow.

Yes, he owed her everything. He could never turn her down.

After a shower, he shook Tim awake. "We're going to church."

Tim threw back the sheet. "Terrific," Tim said as he sat up on the bed, dropped to the floor and stood to stretch. "I've missed church."

"Why didn't you say something?" Mike never knew what his brother was thinking. Of course, Tim never talked about stuff that was important to him. They were a lot alike that way.

"I like sleeping in, too."

At ten forty-five, the cousins were seated together in the sanctuary. Bowing his head, Mike hoped to be filled with the peace this time of silent meditation used to bring him, but it still eluded him. Maybe he was out of practice. Maybe he'd missed too many services. Whatever the reason, the Spirit didn't fill him. He had a feeling it wasn't the Spirit's fault.

He prayed for his family and patients. He knew those requests had been heard, but when he prayed for guidance for himself he felt cold and alone.

Where was God when he needed him so much?

After church, Mike pulled the car into the drive of Francie's house and stopped.

"Why don't you come in?" Francie said as Tim got out of the backseat. "You can make some sandwiches and bring me one." She took Tim's extended hand to get out of the car. Once standing, she went around to the driver's side, opened the door, grabbed Mike's arm and pulled him toward the house.

Once inside, she yawned and said, "I'm going to bed. Would you fix us lunch?" She'd taken a few steps down the hall when she turned to say to Mike, "Before you do that, come with me to look at the baby's room. Brandon painted it last week, and I added a few touches."

Mike followed her down the hall and stopped to look into the bright yellow nursery. On the walls, Francie had hung pictures of whimsical animals in both brilliant and pastel hues. His mother would love this, would want to add a few fanciful ideas of her own.

For a minute, Mike was overwhelmed by the memory of how he and Cynthia had planned to have three children. Their babies could have had a room like this. Well, knowing Cynthia, she wouldn't have liked purple dragons or turquoise birds, but they would have had a nursery. When he noticed Francie studying him, he said, "It's great."

"Hey, Mike, how do you turn on a gas stove?" Tim called.

"Don't do a thing. I'll be right there." Mike pulled himself from his reverie to hustle to the kitchen. If he allowed Tim to light the stove, he might have to explain to Brandon where he'd been when Tim blew up the house.

After he took a tray back to Francie, Mike settled in Brandon's chair in the living room. In no time, he was asleep.

"Hey, Fuller." Dr. Ramírez caught him in the hall outside the E.R. the next evening. "Sorry if I intruded yesterday. I didn't mean to invade your privacy, but…" She bit her lip. "Anyway, I'm sorry."

"Thank you." It was hard to hold a grudge against her. Mike figured she'd be angry if he told her she was so attractive any man would forgive her for anything. And that lip-biting part was distracting. Very distracting.

When Mike moved back toward Trauma 3, he saw Mitchelson watching Dr. Ramírez as she walked away.

"How'd the cup of coffee go?" the nurse asked with a grin. "Was that all? Just a cup of coffee?"

"Just a cup of coffee. She wanted to talk about my work as an orderly."

"Did she tell you that you should be a doctor or nurse?"

Mike glared at Mitchelson. "How did you know she said that?"

"Because we all think so. Can't figure out why you're not in med school, but we're glad we got you in the E.R. and hope you won't leave anytime soon." When his beeper went off, Mitchelson hurried away before Mike could say a word.

"Thank you," he shouted down the hall. Mitchelson waved back.

"Fuller," Dr. Ramírez called in her doctor voice. "Transfer, please."

Back to normal. No more compliments, only a lot of lifting and hard work.

Three days later his mother's bus arrived at 10:00 a.m. which gave Mike plenty of time to clean up after his shift and drive to the bus station.

Before she went to prison, Mom had looked like her paintings: full of life and sparkle, happiness shining from her. She'd changed during those years. Hard to remain vibrant in prison, she'd explained on his frequent visits, as if he couldn't guess that.

He waited on the platform, surrounded by the noise and the strong fumes from diesel engines.

When she got off the bus, he hugged her, noticing she was thinner than he'd remembered.

She pulled away to study him and put her hand on his cheek. "It's so good, so absolutely marvelous to be here," she whispered. "I can't believe I'm out of prison and back with my boys."

"I'm glad, too, Mom."

She still had an innocent face, which had helped her market her forgeries but hadn't fooled the judge. Now her skin bore lines and wrinkles, but the beauty remained.

After she pointed out her one shabby suitcase, Mike handed the baggage claim to the bus driver and carried it to the car.

"I'm so tired of wearing trousers." His mother smoothed her jeans. "Boring, boring, boring, my dear, and not at all feminine." She glared at her white shirt. "Do you still have my dresses?"

"Yes, Francie stored everything while you were gone." Mike started the car and backed out of the parking place. "But it's been eight years. They're probably out of style."

"Good clothing never goes out of style."

He grinned as her sudden air of certainty and confidence. Yes, it was great to have her home.

After he stopped at several lights, she said, "My, my, the traffic is even worse than before." She chattered on about how things had changed in Austin while he drove.

When he pulled up in front of the small house, she said, "What's this? We aren't living here, are we?"

"I know it's not very big, but it's what I can afford."

The shrubbery needed to be trimmed, but the house appeared neat enough on the outside. With white paint that flaked only in a few areas, black shutters, and a porch the size of a postage stamp, it had a homey aspect. But it was small, a fact even more evident when his mother opened the front door and stepped inside.

The living room held a short sofa, two folding chairs and a television on an ugly metal stand. "It came furnished," he explained.

But she didn't notice the furniture when she saw the paintings she'd forged, the ones Francie had saved for her, covering the walls. His mother had loved the impressionists and these glowed with the brilliance of color and light, illuminating the room. She turned to take them in, reaching out her arms to bathe in the beauty. Then she walked slowly toward one and touched her fingers to the rough surface.

"Oh, thank you," she said. "I'd forgotten how much I love these."

After a few minutes, she shook herself and

walked through the rest of the house. First, she wandered back to the kitchen which had maybe five feet of counter space, a few cabinets and a card table with three wobbly chairs.

"I fix most of the meals in the microwave," Mike said.

"Then I'll do the cooking," Mom said.

"I gave you the master—well, the larger—bedroom." He led her toward the door, shoved it open and followed her in to put the suitcase on the bed.

She turned to consider the double bed, one dresser and bare walls. "White," she said. "All the walls are white."

"Tim and I can paint them. You choose the color."

"Thank you. I'd like that." She left the room and looked into the bathroom and the other bedroom. "You and Mike both sleep in here?"

"We'll be fine, Mom. We're brothers. We'll get to know each other better after the years apart."

She nodded again as he followed her back to her bedroom.

"This is a nice part of town. There's an H-E-B grocery store only a block from here. It's an easy walk. And there's a park nearby."

She placed her hand on his arm and patted it. "Mike, this is fine. I appreciate you opening your house to us. We've been apart so long. I'm glad we're together." She smiled and for a moment it was her old smile. "You're a good brother and a fine son." She dropped her hand. Opening the suitcase, she placed her things in a small pile on the bed before she opened the closet.

When she saw what was inside, she pulled out one dress, sat on the end of the bed and stared into the closet. In her lap she held a gown of brilliant green with a shimmering pattern of gold. Tears streamed down her cheeks.

"My clothes," she said. "All of my favorite things are here. Thank you." She stood and embraced Mike.

When Mike opened a drawer in the dresser to show her the jewelry Francie had kept and a small bottle of his mother's favorite perfume he'd bought for her, she cried harder.

"Thank you, son. You've given me a wonderful homecoming."

Oh, boy. Too much emotion for him. When the phone rang, he gave his mother an awkward pat on her back. "I'll get that." He pulled away but touched her shoulder, which seemed to satisfy her. Then he ran into the living room and grabbed the receiver.

"Yes, I can come in early today," he said as he checked his watch. "I'll be in by three."

He hung up the phone, placed his hand on one of the paintings and closed his eyes. With his mother here, the house was filled with turbulence. He could feel it—the tingle of her strong personality, the scent of her musky perfume, the rough swipes of paint in the painting under his fingers.

Yes, Hurricane Tessie had hit. As calm as she seemed today, his mother was always a force to be reckoned with.

He'd let her settle in today, but tomorrow he'd have to talk to her about getting a job to satisfy the conditions of her parole and because they just plain needed that income.

He thought how tired and how much older she'd looked when she got off the bus, about her joy at seeing her clothes and her art. Then he shook his head as he remembered her tears. His mother never cried.

Maybe he'd wait a few days before he suggested she find work.

Chapter Three

Almost midnight a few days later, and a moment of quiet during a long shift in the E.R.

Mike headed outside and leaned back against the wall of the hospital. He took a deep breath, held it and let it out. Sometimes he was overwhelmed by the smell and the stress of the E.R. Tonight it was more than he could handle. After a few minutes and more cleansing breaths, he turned to go inside, walking back through the waiting room and the door into the E.R.

"When did you come in today?" Williams, the big orderly, asked as he pushed an empty gurney.

Stretching, Mike answered, "Three."

"Double shift, huh? You must need the money."

"Don't we all?" He covered a yawn before he went back into Exam 5 to clean the empty room.

"Why are you doing that?" Williams said. "Housekeeping's supposed to do that."

"Because they're running behind and I don't have anything else to do."

"You make us all look bad." Williams headed toward the central desk.

As he dumped the paper bed cover in the trash, Mike realized how beat he was after nine hours of the double shift. With his mother back home, Mike could work longer hours because he didn't have to worry about Tim. Before her arrival, Mike had covered only the night shift, eleven to seven. That way he could get his brother dinner, make sure Tim got up in the morning, and push him out to look for a job. Hard to do all that between a couple of naps.

Now Mike could work more hours to cover his mother's expenses until she got work. Maybe earn enough to catch up with the bills.

"You said last week your mother was coming back to Austin. How's that going?" Mitchelson came into the room.

"Okay. She got here Wednesday and is settling in." He pulled on a new pair of gloves and began disinfecting the counters.

"Where was she?"

"The women's prison in Burnet." When he

turned to throw a paper towel into the bin, he saw Dr. Ramírez standing next to the curtain. Her mouth was open a little. She had obviously heard what he'd said.

Actually, it was a good thing she'd caught the conversation. She might as well know he wasn't the man she thought he was. Maybe she'd stop nagging him and leave him alone. A mother in prison wouldn't fit into her idea of what a doctor should be or the kind of man she'd date.

A man she'd date? Where had that thought come from? The one cup of coffee last week hadn't been an invitation, wasn't meant to be a date of any kind. No, there wasn't any chance of a relationship between them other than doctor-orderly. But, even if the smallest possibility of that existed, the information about his mother would completely scuttle it. An ex-con in the family tended to do that.

"Transfer, Fuller." Dr. Ramírez moved back to the other operating room.

Five minutes later, the injured from an automobile accident and two gunshot victims came in. All needed immediate stabilization and surgery.

He was working calmly until he saw one of the injured was a four-year-old girl, her pink T-shirt smeared with blood and her leg at an angle he didn't like. He forced himself to grin at her as he untied her little sneakers. They had kittens on them, kittens covered with blood.

"Hey, kid," he said. "My name's Mike. Your shirt says you're Naomi."

"My leg," she whispered. "Hurts. A lot."

"I bet it does, buddy. The doctor will be out in a few minutes. She'll help you."

"Fuller," Dr. Ramírez called.

Mike started to move away when Naomi grabbed his hand. "Don't go," she said.

"I'll be back as soon as I can." He wished he had something to give Naomi to keep her company. He took a clean towel, tied it in a knot and handed it to Naomi. "This is Whitey, the friendly polar bear who lives in the hospital and keeps little girls company."

Naomi took the towel and hugged it.

"Nicely done, Fuller," Dr. Ramírez said from the doorway. "Have you thought about working in pedes?"

He faced her. "Need a transfer?"

"Yes." Dr. Ramírez strode toward Naomi then gently pushed the hair from the child's forehead. "Move this gurney into Exam 4 and take her mother upstairs."

By 5:00 a.m., the hospital had quieted again.

He'd transferred four victims to the operating room then to their rooms once they came out of recovery. And he'd taken one body to the morgue. His least favorite transport.

Not a hard night in the E.R., but two shifts added up to a backache and the need to relax for a few minutes. He wished he had time for a nap, but when he got to the break room, another orderly snored on the sofa.

He took a thermos from his locker and poured the last of the coffee into his cup. With a groan, he settled down in the only comfortable chair in the room and leaned his head back.

Barely a few breaths short of falling asleep, he opened his eyes to see Dr. Ramírez put a can of soda on the table and drop in the chair across from him. She seemed to be favoring her right leg and was rubbing her thigh almost surreptitiously.

"Old football injury," she said with a slight smile before she nodded at his thermos and asked, "Saving money?"

"I can't take the coffee someone makes in the E.R."

"I know." She held up her Coke. "Tastes like it's spiked with old motor oil."

"My mother makes terrific coffee. I'd rather have it than pay for it in the cafeteria."

"I heard you say your mother is home from prison."

He nodded and shifted in the chair.

"What was she in for?"

"Forgery."

"Checks?"

"Paintings."

"Oh, an artist." She took a drink of Coke. As she lifted her chin, Mike watched a wisp of hair that had come loose to curl on her neck. He'd never thought of Dr. Ramírez as having curls or long hair…and he'd better *not* think about that.

She put the can down and licked her top lip with the tip of her tongue. The motion wasn't meant to be seductive, just cleaning up after the last drop, but all Mike could think of for a few seconds was her lips, round and soft and pink. She'd spoken for several seconds before Mike realized she'd said something.

"I'm sorry. I'm falling asleep. What did you say?"

"My uncle was in prison." She stood and put the can in the recycle bin.

"Oh?" He swiveled to look at her.

"It was really hard on his family."

That was all she said. She didn't offer sympathy or platitudes or advice or dig further into his life. She only commented on a shared experience. And she didn't say, "I know how you feel." Because no one really did.

"Thank you."

"Fuller," came a male voice from the hall. "Transfer."

"And the fun keeps on coming," Dr. Ramírez said. She gave Mike a smile, that little smile that was only a curving of her lips. It made the long shift seem not nearly as bad.

Ana stretched and massaged the muscles in her neck. She hated the night shift, but that was what she had to cover if she wanted to learn everything she could about emergency medicine.

Besides, her schedule wasn't all that bad: on twenty-four hours, off twenty-four, with no more than seventy hours a week. It allowed her time with her family, time to study and a few hours to rest.

The pain in her thigh was worse than it had been for years. She must have twisted her leg. Now all she wanted to do was elevate it for a few hours. Not an easy thing to do in the E.R.

In the long run, she was sorry she'd heard the conversation between Fuller and the other orderly. Better for her not to know about the private lives of anyone she worked with.

So why *was* she interested in Fuller? Had she

made him her project of the year? Usually her projects were easier to handle, more open and not nearly as attractive as Fuller. Wait. When had she started to think of Fuller as attractive?

Well, what woman wouldn't? He had great longish dark hair and a terrific smile, although few people over the age of ten saw it. What she usually saw was a face clear of expression with a hint of anger in the depths of his dark eyes. The charm and the anger made him, well, interesting, as if he had dimensions he never shared.

Add to that his broad shoulders, great build and the black stubble that covered his chin and cheeks by the end of the shift, and—*¡caramba!*—what's not to like?

Which meant it was time to get back to the E.R. before she had any more completely unprofessional thoughts about a man with no ambition. Maybe in other people's minds, Fuller wouldn't be seen as lacking in ambition. He worked hard, made good decisions, was great with kids. On the other hand, as an orderly he wasn't using every bit of his ability. Why wasn't he in school? Her brothers always told her she was an education snob, and maybe she was, but she hated it when people didn't push themselves to live up to their potential.

Besides that, he was a man who had clearly but

politely told her to leave him alone, a man she had absolutely no interest in.

None at all.

"Hey, *chica*," Enrique, Ana's sixteen-year-old brother, said as she entered her family's home that evening. "What's for dinner?"

"What does it matter, Quique? You eat everything I put on the table. You'd eat lizards if I could catch enough to fill you up." She grabbed him in a hug that became a wrestling match when he tried to slip away.

"Sounds good."

"And you never put on a pound." Ana glanced at his skinny body then down at her rounder hips. "I don't think we come from the same family."

She headed for the kitchen and glanced back at him. "Where are you going?" As if she didn't know. He was wearing baggy shorts, a Spurs T-shirt and his favorite Nike runners.

"Pickup game at Rolando's."

"Dinner is at seven. Be home." She glared at him, well aware that he'd probably grab a bite with Rolando's family before he meandered home in a few hours. "I'd like to see you sometime."

"*Mira.*" He held out his arms and rotated slowly in front of her. "Look, here I am."

"Just go." She waved as he ducked out the door. "Ana, is that you?"

Hearing her father's voice from the kitchen, she hurried toward it. "Hi, Papi."

Her father sat at the table doing a crossword puzzle. He and Enrique looked so much alike. Both six feet tall and slender. Her father had streaks of white in his still-full, dark hair. Before her mother's death almost a year ago, he'd been a quiet and often moody man. Since then, he'd retreated deeper, lost any spring in his step and his shoulders were more rounded. He was still a handsome man but not a happy one, as much as he tried to hide it.

"What's a five-letter word for *hackneyed?* Ends in an *E.*"

"How 'bout *stale* or *trite?*"

"Those might fit." His pen hovered over the folded newspaper.

She pulled an apron from the pantry, tied it around her, and continued to watch her father. He was always doing puzzles. Crossword and Sudoku and anagrams. He had a basket by his chair with puzzle books in it and spent most of his time at home solving those puzzles. He'd become a hermit.

"Papi, you have to get out more." She picked up a dishrag and squirted detergent on it. "Let's go to a movie next Saturday."

He didn't answer, just stared at the crossword clues.

The kitchen cabinets were dark walnut; the linoleum floor that was supposed to look like bricks was well-worn. This place felt a lot more like home than the tiny efficiency she'd recently rented a few blocks from the hospital and spent so little time in. She squeezed out the dishrag and started cleaning the white tile counters.

When she finished, she said, "I thought I'd fix enchiladas tonight." She pulled down a jar of tomato sauce. Her mother had always made her sauce from scratch, with real tomatoes, but this would just have to do. Except for her father, no one could tell the difference. After eating his wife's cooking for thirty-five years, he knew homemade sauce from canned.

Ana's philosophy about cooking was if she covered every dish with cheese and onion, they tasted great. Well, not flan, of course. Because her father was diabetic, she used low fat cheese and watched his portions although he did pretty well keeping track himself.

"Who's going to be here tonight?"

Her father stood, held on to the back of the chair before he walked across the room. He was only sixty-one but appeared much older. A day at the store wore him out now. She'd made him go to the doctor but he said nothing was wrong with her father, not physically. How long did it take to recover from the death of a wife? Obviously, a year wasn't enough.

"Robbie and Martita are coming with Tonito and the baby. She said she'd bring a cake," he said.

"Luz, Quique and Raúl also?" Ana listed the other siblings who lived in Austin. Her brother Robbie, his wife and their small family were fun to be around, and Martita made wonderful cakes. "I want to be sure so I can make enough enchiladas for everyone and still leave some for your lunch Saturday." If Quique didn't eat them when he went through the refrigerator later.

"Well, Raúl will probably stop by. He's between gigs."

Raúl was always between gigs. Fortunately, he had a steady job at the family's furniture store Robbie managed. "Is he between girlfriends?"

"I'm never between girlfriends," Raúl said as he came in from the garage.

"Oh, yes, I know. Women always throw themselves at you. Poor dears." Ana pulled tortillas from the fridge. Store-bought tortillas, another shortcut her mother would never have considered.

"*¿Cómo no?* Why not? They can't resist my smile or my guitar."

What was he going to do in the future? Raúl floated through life, making it on his dark good looks, great smile and personality, plus a dab of talent.

"Hey, Ana, *no te preocupes.* Don't worry."

"Why would I worry about you?" She took out a slab of white cheese and began to grate it.

"Because you always worry about me and Luz and Quique. We're all young." He pulled one of his guitars from the hall closet and came into the kitchen. "We'll grow up someday."

Ana rolled her eyes. "I hope so."

"We'll never be as responsible as you are." He ran his fingers over the strings. "After all, you were born responsible, but you don't *always* have to worry about us."

"Yes, she does, Raúl." Her brother Robbie followed his five-year-old son, Tonito, into the kitchen and placed a cake on the counter. "That's what Ana does. Worries about her family. She's a rescuer."

"Someone has to do it," Robbie's wife, Martita, said. "It's a full-time job. I refuse to take it on." She handed Marisol, the baby, to Robbie and sat at the kitchen table. "But sometime, *chica,* you are going to have to stop taking care of your family and find a life of your own."

A life of her own? An interesting concept. Taking care of her family was, well, habit—one she'd never tried to break until she realized how dependent her father was getting on her. That, and the short drive from her little efficiency to the hospital were the reasons she'd moved. Not one to make changes easily, she felt this one was enough for now.

"You want a date?" Raúl said. "I could fix you up with some guys."

"Thank you," Ana said politely, but she'd never take him up on that. Although she was only twenty-eight, all his friends were *years* younger than she in both age and maturity.

"Don't ever go out with any of his friends," Robbie said. "None of them are serious about anything."

"Why don't you come to church with us?" Martita said. "There's a big singles' group there."

Ana smiled but didn't answer. Other than weddings and funerals, she'd seldom been to church, although Martita had often invited her to the community chapel her family attended. Ana'd never consider going to church only to find a date. It didn't seem quite right to her.

After dinner, they gathered in the family room to sing "Adelita" and "De colores" and other family favorites. Raúl and Quique sat on the bench by the fireplace and strummed their guitars. Her father leaned back in his blue recliner while Martita held her kids on the other recliner, the one Ana's mother had always sat in. Everyone else relaxed on the sofa while Tonito played with his trucks on the floor.

As she watched, Ana was filled with love and with a terrible feeling that this was to be her life: to watch while her brothers and sister married and had babies and the babies grew up and married. And through those years, she'd worry about them, every one of them, exactly as Raúl and Robbie said she would. Forever. She knew that about herself, too.

Sometimes, like now, she wanted more. Now that she'd reached her professional goal, she needed to look ahead. What she wanted now was a family of her own.

Odd—she hadn't thought about marriage for a long time, not since high school when Tommy Schmidt had wanted to marry her after graduation. Her drive to be a doctor had broken up their relationship. There hadn't been anything serious since. Oh, she'd dated, but she'd been so wrapped up in her family, in her push to finish medical school and her need to learn everything she could, to be the best doctor possible, to finish the residency, that she'd never found time for a relationship. Hadn't really wanted one.

Now that she was almost there, what would she do?

Was it too late for her to have a life and family of her own? If she did, she was going to have to leave the warm, comfortable circle of her family and enter the world of dating. The whole idea bothered her. She wasn't good at flirtation or chatter, and her intensity frightened men.

Then the image of Mike Fuller's unsmiling face danced in her brain. As much as she tried to force his image away, she couldn't. As far as she could tell, she didn't intimidate him.

She could not, would not even consider him. How many times did she need to remind herself he was too young for her? No, that was an excuse. How old was he? Twenty-two, twenty-three? Six or seven years wasn't that much of an age difference.

But there were other reasons. To her, he seemed unmotivated and that bothered her, a lot. And he was so guarded, so wary and uncommunicative.

No, Fuller wasn't the man for her, but, well, other than Raul's friends he was the only unmarried man under fifty she knew.

Chapter Four

What really scared Mike was that he could always tell when Dr. Ramírez was in the hospital. He knew when he walked into the E.R.—without even seeing her—if she was there. He didn't understand how this happened. It couldn't be the scent of her perfume because she didn't wear any.

So how did he know?

He refused to believe in psychic phenomena, but every time he spotted her in the E.R. for the first time in a shift, it didn't surprise him.

If he wanted to know for sure, her schedule wasn't hard to figure out. She worked three of seven nights each week. Sometimes he thought about going to the nurses' station and trying to glance at her schedule. Inconspicuously of course because staff was always around.

Besides, the idea of actually planning this and carrying it out felt a little strange, as if there was actually something between the two of them, a relationship of some kind. He shuddered. After Cynthia and with the uncertainty of his life now, even the word scared him. No, there wasn't a relationship between him and Dr. Ramírez, and he could never consider the possibility.

Nevertheless, when he walked in that day at 3:00 p.m. for a double shift, he knew she was there.

Ana gently probed the leg of the crash victim. She couldn't feel anything odd. Of course, the swelling didn't allow for a complete manual examination. "X-ray," she shouted and turned to glance over her shoulder.

He was there. Fuller. Getting ready to transfer the victim to a gurney so the other orderly could push the gurney of another patient into its place.

His presence made her feel a little giddy.

Get a grip, she lectured herself.

"Dr. Ramírez," said an RN. "You have another patient."

"Thanks, Olivia." She dried her hands and held them out for the nurse to slide the clean gloves on her.

The entire night passed in the same way, patient

after patient rolling in, being attended to, then moving on. Between those emergencies, she enjoyed the tantalizing glimpses of Fuller transporting patients or checking with an EMT or picking up a patient's chart. As she did with everyone, she nodded to him or thanked him or got out of his way so he could take the gurney to surgery or a room. At midnight, her aching back forced her to lean against the wall and stretch her muscles. Fuller hurried past, this time giving her a smile, much to her surprise.

He had a great smile. Too bad she didn't see it more. Or, maybe it was a good thing. If he smiled more often, she might behave more foolishly, if that were possible.

During a lull a few hours later, she decided to take a nap. She had two choices. The first: she could hurry over to the on-call rooms on the fifth floor of the east wing. Narrow little places, each with a bed and little else. The problem was, every time she took off her shoes, settled in the bed and pulled the covers over her, her cell rang. Walking all the way over there wasn't worth the trouble.

So she decided on the second choice. She headed for the sofa in the break room and hoped she didn't have to pull rank to get it. Fortunately, she got there first. When she was almost asleep,

the door swung open. She knew it was Fuller.
How? She still couldn't figure it out.

She opened her eyes a slit to see if she was
right. She was.

As she watched, he stepped into the room and
watched her with a gentle expression, one that
didn't fit the Fuller she knew, the Fuller who seldom
spoke to her. It must be the dim light that allowed
the deviant thought that Fuller might look at her in
that way, caring and—oh, certainly not—tender.

After a few seconds, he backed out and closed
the door silently. She sat up. What had just
happened? Quickly she halted the absurd tangent
her brain had taken off on. Tenderness in Fuller's
eyes? Ridiculous.

She had to stop thinking about the orderly. It
was not professional. He was not the man for her.

But something inside her didn't agree, and she
was left to wonder why he'd looked at her like that.

Driving home, Mike could barely keep his eyes
open. Not the safest thing to do when he was
driving, but the extra money from those long
double shifts allowed him to breathe more easily.
For the first time since college, he had a small
savings account. For the first time in weeks, he felt
there might be better times ahead that didn't

consist of constant work, that held the promise he might be a doctor someday.

Not that doctors had easy lives, but they had partners to trade off with, got paid a good bit more and didn't have to do the scut work.

"Orderly," he imagined himself saying in some far-off day when he was Michael Robert Fuller, M.D. "Transport this patient to X-ray, then check on the woman bleeding in Trauma 8. And while you're there—" He almost smiled. Life was getting better when he could see a little humor in the situation, when he felt there might be a future for him in medicine.

He turned onto his street in time to see Tim ride away in his friend's car. Where were they going? He didn't have a job yet. He'd ask Tim later where he'd gone, if he remembered, but he wasn't worried. This was too early in the day to get in trouble, even for Tim.

Pulling Francie's car into the drive, he got out and stretched. He waved down the street toward the neighborhood kids waiting for the school bus as he walked across the lawn and onto the porch. It was hot already, even though it was only late May. That was central Texas.

He unlocked the front door, shoved it open and took a step inside. Silence surrounded him, the usual situation with Tim gone except normally his mother was drinking coffee and reading the paper in the kitchen when he got home. Today the door of her bedroom was shut and a line of light glowed from beneath it. Was she sick?

He knocked and said, "Mom, are you okay?"

When she threw the door open, the dazzling light from her smile and several lamps made him blink.

"I'm magnificent, dear. Look at this." She swirled and gestured around her.

The blast of brilliance made him stand still for a moment. Then he took three steps inside and blinked in an effort to take the scene in.

On the wall to his left, his mother had painted a view of a meadow with two women walking through it. Vibrant green grass and a dazzling sky filled the entire area. On the wall in front of him, she'd begun to paint a pond with gauzy water lilies floating on its shimmering surface.

Wearing one of his shirts and old jeans smeared with paint, his mother stood in the middle of an amazing blaze of beauty.

"I see you're Claude Monet today," he said stunned by the joy in his mother's face and the glow of the painting on the walls. Mixed with all this was the realization this was a rental house for which he'd signed an agreement: all plans to paint had to be approved by the landlord. He didn't think the landlord would appreciate the swirling glory on the walls, but it was too late to worry now. He and Tim could paint over it before they moved out.

Walking to the center of the room, he allowed the paintings to fill him with joy. "When did you decide to do this?"

"After you left yesterday afternoon, I took a walk." While she talked, she picked up a paper towel and wiped the plate she'd used as a palette. "There's a wonderful art store only three block from here. Did you know that?" She glanced up at him with a smile, the kind he remembered from when he was a kid.

He dropped on the bed to listen.

"They had a bin of old paint really cheap, so I bought some and a few brushes, and, well, everything I needed. It cost almost nothing." She turned in a slow circle to study her creations. "Once I got started, I couldn't stop. I painted the rest of the day and all night, stopped to feed Tim dinner and breakfast then came back here." With a sigh, she put the plate down and sat next to him on the bed.

"I didn't know how much I missed it. The painting." Her eyes shone. "Not until I put the first stroke of color on the wall and inspiration flowed through me. It kept coming and coming, like it had been locked up inside me all these years."

"You painted for twenty hours?"

"Almost." She smiled. "It was wonderful. It was like coming home, coming home to you and Tim and my painting." She stood to twirl in the middle of the room.

Mike pulled himself off the bed. "I'm glad, Mom. It's great."

"Thank you, dear." She patted his cheek. "Now, let me get you some breakfast. We can eat together. Then I have to take a nap. Although," she said, "my brain is so filled with images, I don't know if I can sleep."

"Mom, it's beautiful. What's next? Another Monet? Degas's dancers? Seurat?"

"Never Seurat. I find painting all those little dots so tedious."

She was happy. He'd let her finish her bedroom, which wouldn't take long at the speed she was going. *Then* he'd help her find a job.

Almost a week later, his mom still hadn't found work although she'd made several calls and filled out lots of applications. On the other hand, a Degas dancer stretched her long right leg across one corner in the kitchen. In the hall, the start of his mother's interpretation of a Pisarro view of a street made Mike feel as if he were walking through Paris. The landlord might be able to use the house as a gallery or charge higher rent with all the art filling it.

"Fuller, there's a kid in the E.R. who needs you," Dr. Armstrong said, interrupting Mike's thoughts.

In the past few weeks, Mike had gotten a reputation for being good with kids. This was good because he liked children, but bad because he really hated to see a kid hurt.

After finding the child, comforting her and getting her prepped for surgery, he transported her to the OR and promised he'd be there when she got out of surgery.

A few hours later, Mike glanced at his watch. Almost 6:00 a.m. His mother would be picking him up after the shift change. She'd needed the car to go to the doctor yesterday afternoon, only a routine visit, she'd said. He hoped everything had gone well.

Because he'd expected her to arrive an hour later, seeing her in the E.R. hallway surprised him. Even more amazing, she supported a gray-haired man with one hand and tried to staunch the blood dripping from the towels wrapped around the man's arm with the other.

"Mom?"

"Hello, dear." She gave him a quick smile. "I met Mr. Ramírez in the parking lot and helped him in." She lowered the man into a chair. "He says his daughter works here. Do you know her?"

"Yeah." Mike pulled gloves from his pockets, slipping them on as he ran to the nurses' station. "Page Dr. Ramírez, please." Then he grabbed a couple of towels from a hall cabinet, dropped the blood-soaked towels from Mr. Ramírez's arm on the tile floor and wrapped the clean ones around it. Before he could do more, Dr. Ramírez rushed toward her father.

"Papi, what is it?" She kneeled in front of him and glanced at the already-bloody towels. "Fuller, get a wheelchair and take my father to—" she checked the whiteboard "—Trauma 2."

"I don't need a wheelchair." Mr. Ramírez pulled himself to his feet and took a step.

Dr. Ramírez didn't say a word, just gave her father the look that stopped orderlies in their tracks or had them leaping to do what she expected. He sat.

"Marvin," she said to the clerk, "check my father in and get housekeeping here stat to clean the area and get rid of the towels."

Mike pulled his gloves off and dropped them in a closed bin. "Mom, get some soap from Marv and wash your hands and arms and face really well. Scrub hard."

Then he helped Dr. Ramírez's father into the wheelchair and pushed him to the desk where the older man handed his insurance information to Marvin.

"Marv, I'll get you the rest of the info in a minute. I need to check on my father." Dr. Ramírez grabbed the chair and wheeled it into the cubicle. "Fuller, transfer."

Once her father was lying on the examining table, Dr. Ramírez started to unwrap the arm. "How did you do this, Papi?"

"I was trimming the hedge—"

Mike took the wheelchair away as nurses and an intern and other personnel crowded into the trauma bay.

"Papi, you know you should leave those jobs for one of the boys to do," Mike heard her say as he left.

"I'm not a baby, Ana. I can do this."

"Papi," Dr. Ramírez said. "You always think you're so macho, invincible."

When Mike left the wheelchair in the corridor, he reminded himself to have housekeeping clean it well. He entered the waiting room, and his mother looked up at him.

"How is he? Will he be all right?"

"I don't know, but he has the best doctor in the

place taking care of him. I'll check in with her later and let you know." He sat in the green plastic chair next to her and took a hand that was still a little damp. "Why are you here so early?"

"I was going to eat breakfast in the cafeteria and be here when you got off."

"Well, go ahead." He reached into a pocket for a bill. "Get some breakfast."

"No, no. I don't feel like it now. I'll wait here."

"Then tell me what happened. You found him in the parking lot?"

"Yes. Poor man, he drove himself here. I saw him getting out of the car. He almost fell and his face was white." She fanned out the skirt of her long, gauzy mauve dress before she stared at the dark smears on it. "I didn't realize I was getting bloody. What should I do?" She glanced up at Mike. "I should change clothes."

"I'm worried. I'm sure he's a nice man, but blood can carry infections like hepatitis, which would be dangerous for you."

"I know, Mike, but I couldn't leave the poor man to lie on the pavement."

Of course she couldn't, despite the risk. "I'll get you a set of scrubs."

She straightened. "Scrubs?" She bit the words off with obvious distaste.

"I know they aren't your usual style, but scrubs are all we have. They're better than what you're wearing."

She nodded. "All right. I'll try scrubs."

"You'll make them look good."

As he stood, Dr. Ramírez entered the waiting room. Approaching his mother, she reached out her hand. "I'm Dr. Ramírez. I can't thank you enough for helping my father."

"I'm Tessie Fuller, Mike's mother." She got up. "I was glad to help. I can't believe your father drove himself here."

"What can I say?" Dr. Ramírez shrugged. "He thinks he can do anything."

"How is he?" His mother grabbed Dr. Ramírez's arm as she spoke.

"Dr. Price, a surgeon, is stitching up the arm. That won't take long, but we're going to keep him overnight. He lost a lot of blood and would have lost more if you hadn't helped." She nodded at his mother and smiled. "We want to make sure everything is okay before we release him."

"Oh, my, yes. I understand."

"I'm glad to meet you. Thank you again." Then she dropped the smile and said. "Fuller, transfer."

Before he could follow Dr. Ramírez into the E.R., his mother pulled on his hand. "She's a pretty young woman *and* a doctor." She studied Mike's face. "Nice smile. And you work together."

"Yes, Mother." He knew what was coming and tried to pull away.

"She could be the right one."

"Mom, she's a doctor. I'm a med-school dropout which makes her the absolutely wrong one." He pried her hand off his arm and said, "I've got to go back to the E.R., but I'll get you the scrubs when I can."

A long shift change ended at seven-thirty. Wearily, Mike walked into the waiting room carrying a set of scrubs. His mother wasn't there.

Great.

He asked the clerk if she'd seen his mother but she'd just replaced Marv and didn't know her. Maybe Mom had decided to eat breakfast. He'd taken a step toward the hallway when Dr. Ramírez called him from the door to the E.R.

"Fuller."

He turned back.

"Guess who was visiting my father when I checked on him at seven?" She shook her head and smiled.

"My mother?" His stomach tightened. Please, no.

She nodded. "Yep. If you're looking for her, you might try there."

Great. He jogged down the hall, pushed the elevator call button impatiently until the door finally swished open and he got on. His mother collected strays. That was how Francie had come to live with them when her father went to prison, but this stray happened to be Dr. Ramírez's father. The complications of a friendship between them overwhelmed him.

He got off the elevator on the fifth floor and walked down the hall looking for the room number the clerk had given him. When he got there, the door was open. Inside, his mother buttered a piece of toast and held it out for Mr. Ramírez to take a bite. The patient had his arm wrapped and elevated. A monitor was attached while an IV dripped. He had some color back in his face and gazed at his mother with all the interest a man in pain could.

Well, well, well.

After watching for a minute, Mike entered the room. "Mom, do you want these scrubs?"

"Oh, yes, dear." She wiped her hand on a napkin and stood. "I'm sorry, Antonio, but I need to go change now and go home. I'll call to check on you tomorrow." She put a sheet of paper in her pocket. "I have your number."

"Thank you, Tessie." Mr. Ramírez smiled at

her. "Thank you for helping me into the hospital and for feeding me breakfast. Please call."

"Of course, but you take a nap." She followed her son from the room.

"You fed him breakfast?" Mike smiled at her while they waited for the elevator.

"Poor man. He couldn't feed himself with only one arm, now could he? And the aides couldn't help him until much later. His food would have been cold." She put her hand on his arm and nodded, her dangling earrings bouncing with the movement of her head. "I believe it's so important to help others, don't you?"

Just terrific.

Chapter Five

When Ana walked into her father's kitchen the next day, Mrs. Fuller sat at the table with her dad. Ana paused for a minute and tried to think of any reason Mike's mother would be there.

In spite of what her family might say about her, Ana wasn't nosy. At least, not today. She'd dropped by to check on her father and start dinner, but he didn't look as if he needed her care. Which was fine, but she wondered what was going on. After all, the charming widow had spent time with her father while he was in the hospital. Now he'd been home for only a day and here she was again.

Her father held the business section of the newspaper—odd because recently he was only reading the sports page and doing the crossword puzzles. But when she saw the pen in Mrs. Fuller's hand and the pad of yellow paper in front of her, the reason for the rendezvous made sense.

With her nice, conservative black slacks, with a plain black cotton sweater, it was an outfit that looked like something Ana's mother might have worn with a pair of tiny gold earrings and the cross Papi had given her when they married. But Mrs. Fuller accessorized her outfit with a huge red scarf covered in gold swirls tossed around her shoulders. Her gold sandals with red bangles matched it. In greater contrast to Ana's mother, when Mrs. Fuller spoke she waved her hands and light flashed off the jewels of her many rings. The bangles on her wrists jangled and reflected the light coming in the window.

Flamboyant was the word that came to mind. Oh, Mrs. Fuller was lovely, full of energy but so very different from Mama. Sweet, loving, *quiet* Mama.

For a minute she watched them: Mrs. Fuller tapped her pen on the table, which caused her bracelets to clank together. Then she looked at Papi with a smile he returned. He said something to her, and Mrs. Fuller leaned toward him and laughed.

And so, in spite of the differences, Ana couldn't be unhappy. For the first time in over a year, her father was smiling. Mrs. Fuller seemed to pump him up, to delight him, to make him happy, all of which were good. He needed company during the few days Ana had made him stay home from the store. However, there was still the problem with Mrs. Fuller's criminal past, but this was hardly the place to discuss that.

"Hello, Mrs. Fuller. It's nice to see you again," Ana said.

Fuller's mother glanced up at her. "Hello, Doctor. Your father is helping me find a job." She scowled and tapped a pen in frustration. "I'm afraid I have no employable skills."

"Hello, Ana," Papi greeted her. "I was thinking when I go back to the store next week, Tessie could work for me and help with some of the little things. Answer the phone. Take messages."

"Oh, Antonio, really?" Mrs. Fuller's rings glittered when she clapped her hands. "At your store?"

"Sure, I can use the help for a while."

"I could be a gofer, too." Mrs. Fuller clapped, her bangles shimmering in the light from the window. Then she bit her lower lip. "But I don't want to take advantage of your good nature."

"It's a good idea." Ana slid past the table. "I don't want my father to overdo it."

"And it will give you some experience and a reference," Papi said.

"I don't have much experience," Mrs. Fuller

said to Ana. "And no references." She sighed. "I've called fifteen places today, and they aren't interested. Even if I didn't have a record, they wouldn't be interested."

"We'll keep searching," Papi said.

"Oh, thank you, Antonio. I don't know what I'd do without your encouragement."

"Would you like to stay for dinner, Mrs. Fuller?" Ana opened the freezer to pull out a casserole. "We always have plenty of food."

"Please, call me Tessie." She glanced at the kitchen clock. "I didn't realize it was so late. I have to catch a bus and get home in time to fix dinner for the boys." She stood. "But thank you. Please ask me again."

"Has Tim found a job yet?" Papi asked.

"Yes, he's working at Burger Heaven a few blocks from where we live. He started last week." She picked up her tapestry purse and said, "Goodbye, Antonio. Goodbye, Doctor." With a swirl and to the jingling of her bangles, she dashed from the kitchen.

After she heard the front door shut, Ana said, "Papi, are you sure you should be going back to the store so soon?"

He gave her the don't-contradict-me expression he'd perfected years ago and didn't answer. She'd known he wouldn't.

* * *

Ana scrutinized the gunshot wound in the young man's thigh. Not much bleeding because the EMT had cut the trouser leg off and done a good job stanching the flow, but it hurt the patient on the gurney.

"What's your name?" Ana asked.

"Julio Rivera," he said through clenched teeth.

"How did this happen, Mr. Rivera?" Ana asked.

"A car drove by and someone inside shot me."

Ana observed the young man. His light brown complexion was dry, no sweating, no sign of shock, although pain was obvious in his dark eyes. "They're holding an operating suite for you. We'll take you there in a few minutes and will get you pain medication while you're in recovery." She shone her light in his eyes. The pupils were fine. No drugs, no concussion. Not that there would be with a leg wound, but it never hurt to check. Patients didn't always tell doctors everything.

"I don't understand." He shook his head. "I didn't recognize anyone." He closed his eyes. "I was waiting for the bus to go to work, not doing a thing to anyone, when they shot me."

"Gang initiation?" Mike spoke softly from behind her.

Startled by his closeness, Ana looked over her

shoulder. To hide the pleasant flutter seeing him gave her, she said in her professional voice, "Maybe, but now he needs a transfer."

"Yes, Doctor." He moved the gurney around her leaving her to stare at his back as he moved farther away.

"Doctor," Olivia, the nurse, called. "Patient in Trauma 1."

A few hours later, Ana leaned against the wall around the corner from the emergency entrance. Despite the howling of ambulances and the shouts of the medical personnel, it was a peaceful place. At least as peaceful as it got around the hospital with maybe the exception of the chapel. She didn't know because she'd never felt like visiting the place.

Across the lawn was a small garden outside the west wing. If she ignored the noise and focused on the greenery, she could calm herself.

Feeling the approach of Mike, as she was beginning to think of him, she turned toward him. Yes, it was Mike Fuller. How amazing that she knew that. Not wanting to examine the phenomenon that made her a little breathless, she said as she watched his approach, "I didn't know you came here."

"Yeah," he said with no explanation.

"Did you know your mother visited my father at our home?"

"No." He frowned. "I slept most of the day and came in early."

"When I went to my father's house last night, she was there. He was helping her look for a job. What do you think?"

Mike nodded and leaned against the wall next to her. "What do you think?"

Just like Fuller to answer her question with one of his own. She watched his face but it was blank, no emotion showed anyplace. Here she was with her heart beating faster and longing to get some reaction from him, but the man never gave anything away.

"He hasn't smiled so much since my mother died last year."

"That's not what I meant." He dropped his gaze to his feet. "I mean how do you feel about your father seeing an ex-con?"

"I don't know." She considered her words. "Actually, I do. It bothers me because I don't know your mother, but this is my father's decision. I know better than to interfere in what my father does." She sighed. "If she makes him happy, I'll accept it. I'll be glad for both of them."

For almost a minute she watched Mike's hands on the top of the wall, powerful hands with thick, strong fingers. Finally she looked up to meet his glance. "What do *you* think of your mother's keeping company with my father?"

He shoved his hands in his pocket. "It's okay."

"They are, after all, adults who have raised families and can make their own decisions." When he didn't answer, she said, "Right?"

He nodded.

She shouldn't care if Mike communicated with her or not. They worked together. There was no reason for her to say much more to him than, "Transfer" and "Thank you" and "Fuller." He did respond well to those, transferring when asked, coming when needed, but not a lot else. She had no right to expect or demand more.

As he moved away, she said, "Let's not allow anything between our parents to affect our work situation."

"Doctor, orderly. Got it." Without another word, he headed back to the E.R.

"That's not—" she started to say but he was already around the corner. Taking a deep breath and attempting to gather enough calm to last the rest of her shift, she followed him into the building a minute later.

Mike strode inside when the automatic doors opened.

What was his mother doing? Keeping company

with Dr. Ramírez's father would make life difficult. It would make *Mike's* life difficult.

When he heard, "Transfer" from the E.R., he hurried down the hall to answer the call, but his mind continued to consider the situation between his mom and Mr. Ramírez.

He could handle being attracted to Dr. Ramírez. He'd deny it, ignore it and work through the situation. That's all there was to it. The buzz he felt when she was around was extremely pleasant but couldn't—wouldn't—lead anywhere. If he allowed it to be any more than that, he was setting himself up for trouble, for a complication he didn't need.

If their families became close, the line between doctor and clinical assistant might blur or even be erased. The thought scared him, a lot.

At the direction of the attending physician, he grabbed a gurney with a patient to transfer to the OR, pushed it toward the elevator and pressed the call button.

As the elevator door opened, he could hear calls of "Transfer" and there were only two orderlies on tonight. Better get moving.

Almost a week later, Mike dropped on the sofa as soon as he got home and fell asleep immediately.

"Antonio has invited us to dinner tonight." His

mother's voice filtered through the shroud of sleep, seeping into his brain, slowly. After trying to make sense of the syllables, their meaning came together. He opened his eyes and muttered, "What? Who? When?" sounding like a high-school journalism teacher. Then he blinked several times, rotated his shoulders, and swung his feet around to sit up. "You're going to Mr. Ramírez's house for dinner?"

Not good. He'd hoped any attraction between his mother and Mr. Ramírez would slowly go away. He'd wished they were just friends, but what he'd seen sparkling between the two of them at the hospital, added to the fact she'd visited Mr. Ramírez in his home and now planned to go to his house for dinner—that added up to more than just the beginning of a friendship.

She sat on the sofa next to him. "We're all going to their house for dinner. You, Tim and I."

He stretched and yawned, trying to think of an excuse.

"I'm sorry I woke you up, but I was so excited."

"I have to work tonight." Work was a terrific reason not to go.

"Not until eleven, right?"

He nodded reluctantly. Could he call now and get on an earlier shift? "Mom, I don't feel comfortable. Dr. Ramírez is my supervisor."

"They're going to have Mexican food." She smoothed his hair away from his face and attempted to pat down his cowlick. "Everyone is bringing a dish. You love enchiladas."

"I don't think mixing work with…"

The smile on her face disappeared. She slumped and bit her lip. "I understand," she said. "I thought how nice it would be for Antonio's family to meet mine, but if you can't make it, I understand. You work very hard for us."

As he watched her, Mike realized how brave his mother had been, flitting around the house as if she had no cares, painting the wonderful scenes, which brightened the entire house, taking care of her sons. All her activity hid the fact she'd only recently been released from eight hard years in prison. She was almost sixty and sometimes looked every day of it and more. As she bent her head, he could see silver streaks threaded through her red hair. She was no longer Hurricane Tessie. She wasn't even Light Breeze Tessie.

Certainly he could do one thing for her.

"All right, Mom. I'll go this time, but don't ask me again, okay?"

"Oh, thank you." She smiled at him, the sparkle returning to her eyes and taking ten years from her age. "Just this one time." She nodded and stood.

Glancing at her watch, she said, "It's barely noon. We need to be there at six, so you have plenty of time to get a nice rest. Go back to sleep."

As if there were any possibility of his getting any more sleep now. He lay on the couch for fifteen minutes, eyes wide-open and staring at the ceiling before he got up and took a shower.

When she'd gotten off her shift the morning of the dinner, Ana had stopped at the grocery store on the way back to her apartment. Only a few blocks from the hospital, her place cost more in rent than an apartment so small should, but she was earning more now and the proximity to the hospital was worth the cost.

She parked her car, got out and took the elevator to the third floor. Once there, she unlocked the door to go inside, dropped her purse on the table in the entry, walked across the tiny patch of beige carpet that was her living room and into the narrow galley kitchen. There, she pulled out the ingredients for the dish she was taking to the dinner.

First she cut the *menudo* into small pieces, put it in a pot with a calf's foot, chilies, bay leaf and garlic, leaving them to simmer while she slept.

When she awakened six hours later, she

checked the *menudo,* added a few more ingredients, then took a shower.

How should she dress tonight? she wondered while she dried her hair.

For goodness' sake, why was she acting all girlie? Tonight was a family dinner, only with a few extra guests. She'd dress as she always did for family dinners: jeans and a T-shirt.

But one of those extra guests was Mike Fuller and, for a reason she refused to admit, she wanted to look better than "okay." She hated the fact he only saw her as a doctor with her funny little bun, lab coat and comfortable shoes. She wanted to break free of the image tonight, to be a real person.

On the other hand, their relationship was doctor-CA so she should choose her clothing accordingly. Having made the decision not to dress in any special or unusual or totally different way for the additional guests, she pulled her hair in a ponytail, slipped into her jeans, shirt and athletic shoes, and studied herself in the mirror.

Plain. Exactly what she looked like. Her younger sister and friends wore makeup, but with her schedule, Ana stayed with a fluff of powder and swipe of lip gloss which was usually gone after a few hours. Did she have anything more in the drawer?

A touch of blush and a dab of mascara made her appear a little prettier. Next she pulled her hair from the scrunchie and brushed it. She liked it curling down her back. Finally, she changed into a yellow cotton blouse with ruffles around the neck and put on matching sandals.

This time when she studied her reflection, she had to admit she looked good, really good. She shook her head to allow the curls to swish across her shoulders.

She was no longer Dr. Ramírez. She was Ana Ramírez, and she was all female.

In the entire city of Austin, how had he ended up in front of *this* house, with Dr. Ramírez inside? His mother would, of course, expect him to enter it. He would have banged his head against the steering wheel in frustration if having to explain the injuries didn't present such difficulty. So instead, he sat in the car with its engine still running in front of the Ramírez's house and thought, *She's in there.*

"Are you getting out?" Tim asked from the backseat. "I don't how you feel about it, but we've been promised Mexican food. I'm not going to miss any of it." He leaped out and loped toward the house.

"Mike," his mother said with concern in her voice, "you don't have to go in if you're uncomfortable."

Uncomfortable wasn't the word he'd use to describe the reluctance he felt.

"Thanks, Mom." But it would be worse if he sat in a car in the drive all evening. They'd think he was more of an idiot than he actually was. He turned off the ignition, got out of the car and went to the other side to help his mother out. Before Mike could reach her, Mr. Ramírez hurried from the house and opened the car door.

"Bienvenida, querida mía," the widower said with a big smile and stretched his arm out for Tessie to take. After she turned in the seat and stood, he kissed her on the cheek.

Dr. Ramírez's father was kissing his mother. That stomach-tightening thing hit him again. Oh, sure, it was on the cheek, but it was a kiss.

How was a son supposed to respond to seeing his mother embraced by a man? Mike had no idea. He'd never thought of Mom as, well, a woman who would be attractive to a man, as a woman a man would want to kiss. Only Tim's running out of the house seconds later saved Mike from standing by the car with his mouth hanging open and looking like a fool.

"Hey, Mike, wanna play some roundball?"

Mike closed his mouth and nodded. He probably would have agreed if Tim had said, "Wanna jump into a pit of cobras?"

"This is Quique," Tim said, pointing to the wiry, good-looking kid holding a basketball who'd followed him. "He says there're some kids down the block always ready for a pickup game." His mother and Mr. Ramírez moved on to the lawn as Tim grabbed the ball from Quique and dribbled it down the sidewalk.

"What about dinner?" Mike asked.

"Ana said I was in the way and kicked me out," Quique shouted as he ran after Tim. "Told us to come back in an hour."

After his brain reminded him Ana equaled Dr. Ramírez, he realized that playing ball would get him out of a situation that could be potentially embarrassing, uncomfortable, better avoided for as long as possible, *or* all of the above.

He slammed the car door on the passenger side, pretended not to notice his mother and Mr. Ramírez holding hands as they strolled toward the house, and followed Tim and Quique down the street.

Ana surveyed the kitchen table in her father's house. The chorizo Martita brought was on the table next to Ana's *menudo*. Rice and *frijoles refritos* flanked those dishes. Her father had made his delicious enchiladas, everything from scratch, the old Mexican way. Her younger sister, Luz, would bring *pan dulce* and salad from the H-E-B where she worked. Even Raúl had brought something, tacos from a Mexican food place. For drinks there were *yerba verde* and soda. Ana would fix the sopaipillas for dessert later.

"What can I do to help?" Mrs. Fuller asked.

"Nothing, thank you. Everything's as ready as possible until Luz gets here." Ana tugged at the corner of the tablecloth to square it.

"Please tell me about Luz. From what Antonio says, she seems like a lovely young woman."

"Yes, she is. She's nineteen. She graduated from high school last year and has been working. A month ago, she decided she'd like to join the army to learn a skill and get financial help for college."

"Sounds like a determined young lady."

"Yes, everyone in our family is determined to reach their goals." She thought of Raúl and Quique. "Well," she added, "almost everyone is."

As she watched Mrs. Fuller sit by her father, Ana wondered where Mike was. She'd seen Tim dash by with Quique, but where was his older brother?

Not that she really cared where he was, but she needed to know so she'd have the correct number of plates set out, enough glasses.

Maybe he'd weaseled out of dinner. *Weaseled,* not an attractive word, but she would've done the same thing if she hadn't promised her father she'd help set up a dinner for friends. Next time, she'd get more information about the guests before agreeing.

Finally, Luz arrived, her dark hair coming loose from the ponytail she wore to work. "Sorry, I had to stay a few minutes late," she said. "Go call Quique and I'll finish setting up. I saw them playing basketball at the Parker's when I drove past."

Ana should have refused the request because when she got to the door, the three guys were heading up the drive. They were all sweaty and their T-shirts clung to their chests. Tim and Quique were skinny and didn't look all that great.

But Mike. Oh, yeah. She had to stop herself from saying, "Wow," as he walked toward her. His shirt stuck to broad shoulders and a muscular torso. Powerful legs showed beneath khaki shorts. Perspiration trickled down his smiling face. He was breathing a little heavily but still laughing and bickering with the two younger guys.

All in all, he looked absolutely spectacular. She'd never seen him look happy and so masculine and would prefer *never* to see him look that great again.

When Mike saw her, he stopped talking. For an instant admiration shone in his eyes as he studied her hair and the ruffled blouse. Then the usual Mike Fuller unemotional face covered his features again.

After the three reached the door, Mike said, "Go on in, guys. I'll follow in a minute." Once the boys shut the door behind them, Mike dropped on the porch bench, leaned over and took deep breaths.

Ana had planned to follow the young men in but his respiration bothered her. She sat next to him, grabbed his wrist and began counting his pulse as she checked her watch. "What's wrong?" she asked. "Do you have any chest pain?"

He tugged his wrist from her hand. "I'm fine." After a few more deep breaths, he added, "Just the idiocy of trying to keep up with kids."

"You're okay?" She sat back. "I thought you were dying." Now that she knew he was fine, Ana attempted not to laugh.

"I did, too, for the last fifteen minutes." He groaned and shook his head. "I haven't played basketball so hard in years."

He sat next to her struggling to breathe with perspiration pouring off him. All in all, he looked better than a man had the right to. She couldn't take her eyes off him.

"Why didn't you stop if you were so tired?" she asked.

"And let the kids win?" He stared at her with an expression that said women just didn't get it. "Besides, it was a lot of fun."

He was right. She didn't get it. How could he think pushing himself to the point of exhaustion was a lot of fun?

She'd never understand men.

Chapter Six

From the swing in the side yard, Ana watched her family and the Fullers. The younger group laughed together in wicker chairs pulled into a semicircle. Martita and Robbie pulled the last of the patio chairs around the big table and talked to Raúl, Papi and Tessie, who sat across from them.

Ana could hear the "rrr" noises Tonito made as he rolled his toy cars across the patio. Baby Marisol played with her toes on a blanket next to her mother.

Mike, the last one out of the house with his plate, stood on the back steps and searched for a place to sit. Glancing at Tim, then away, made it clear he didn't want to sit with the youngsters. Too old for their antics? A glance told him the round table was full and there were no more chairs on the patio.

"There's a seat on the swing." Tessie pointed behind her. Mike smiled at his mother and started in that direction.

At that moment, Ana realized something frightening: Mike was no longer *her* project. She and Mike were their *families'* project. Even worse, she guessed Mike's mother was as persistent as her family. They'd never escape.

As she watched Mike approach her, Ana knew exactly when he realized the seat on the swing, the place his mother had indicated, was next to her, the dreaded Dr. Ramírez. After two steps, his smile slipped and he hesitated. Only for a second, a pause imperceptible to anyone who hadn't been watching him as closely as she had. Almost immediately, he took another step and another until he stood only a few feet from her.

"May I join you?"

At her nod, he put his drink on the table next to the swing and held on to the arm to lower himself onto the cushioned seat. Neither said a word, not a single word, while chatter and laughter from the others floated across the lawn toward them. The fun everyone else was having made their silence even more awkward.

She searched for something to say to fill the quiet that became more uncomfortable by the second. Then her gaze landed on the plate in his lap. "Do you like Mexican food?"

"Yes." He took another bite of the chicken enchilada.

Great conversation.

When he swallowed, she said. "What's your favorite?"

Before she finished her question, he took another bite. Not to let him off the hook, she continued to watch him until he swallowed and said, "Tacos."

"I mean, *real* Mexican food."

"What?" He turned toward her, his forehead creased in confusion. "Tacos are Mexican food."

Success. The response was five words long, and he'd made eye contract. "And you know that because they serve them at Taco Bell?"

He laughed. "Okay, tell me why tacos aren't Mexican food."

Wonder of wonders. A laugh and another complete sentence.

"In Mexico, tacos are like sandwiches," she said. "You put whatever leftovers you have around the house into the taco shell. Fish, vegetables, anything handy."

He shook his head. "I can't imagine eating a fish taco so I'll say my favorite food is this chorizo. I love the spicy sausage."

She was feeling good about the conversation until he added, "Is that answer acceptable, Dr. Ramírez?"

"I didn't mean to sound so much like Dr. Ramírez." She could kick herself for the pedantic streak that showed up at the worst times. "Tonight, while we're all family, why don't you call me Ana. It's more comfortable."

He cleared his throat and glanced away, not acting a bit comfortable.

She'd guess he wouldn't call her anything tonight, most certainly not Ana.

He took a forkful of another food. "Now this is good. It might be my new favorite." He studied the serving on his plate. "What is it?"

"Menudo."

"What's *menudo?*" He took another bite.

"Tripe." When he raised an eyebrow, she said, "That's intestine, beef intestine."

He stopped chewing and looked as if he wanted to spit it out but was too polite.

"If it tastes good, it doesn't matter what it is," she said.

He swallowed and nodded. "I guess so, in theory, at least to a certain extent." He shook his head. "But intestine?"

After a few more minutes of chatter about the food and their families, she decided to try something more risky—digging for information she'd like to know while he was more talkative. "So, Mike, why did you decide to become a doctor?"

He didn't answer. Instead, he gazed at their families and down at his plate until he responded. "All the wrong reasons."

At least he'd answered. She'd figured he'd put up his barrier again. "What are the wrong reasons?"

"Money," he said. "Big house, country club membership so I could play golf on Thursday afternoons. Everything a kid with my background dreams of but doesn't have a chance at."

She pushed the swing slowly, watching the pinks and yellows of the sunset streak the sky before she asked, "So why didn't it work out?"

Ana couldn't believe how quickly his eyes lost every sparkle of interest and became bleak, how his lips thinned and his posture became rigid. He'd thrown up a barrier and glared at her from behind it.

Back to the old Fuller. How frustrating.

"Why did you become a doctor, Dr. Ramírez?" he asked in a voice devoid of interest.

His choice of "Dr. Ramírez" and his asking her the question showed how far she'd trespassed into his territory.

Should she tell him that after the traffic accident her mother was involved in that had nearly take

Mama's life, Ana had admired the skill of the doctors so much she'd vowed to be one? Or should she give him the expanded, emotional reason?

After her mother's accident when Ana was eight years old, she and her father had raced to the hospital, terrified that her mother would die. Ana'd stood on tiptoe to look through the glass into the emergency room. It had been calming to know all the people on the other side of the window were caring for Mama. When Papi had found her, he tried to carry her back to the waiting room, but she'd insisted on staying.

After they'd wheeled her mother to the operating room, she put her arms around his neck and kissed his cheeks. *"No llores,* Papi. *Los doctores le van a salvar la vida."*

He'd quit crying and the doctors had saved her mother's life, but she was *really* sure Mike wouldn't want to hear all the touching details.

"When I was a kid, emergency room doctors saved my mother's life."

He nodded. "That's a good reason." Then he stood. "Coffee?"

"Oh, no." She jumped to her feet. "I have to make the sopaipillas for dessert."

They both went in different directions. Actually, Ana thought they'd fled in different directions because the sharing was more than Mike could handle and she was beginning to feel embarrassed about pushing him to talk.

But no one else would see that. The Ramírezes and the Fullers would feel this had been a successful blending of the families. Only she knew that Mike wasn't ready for the sharing and kidding the Ramírez family did every time they came together.

Because Martita had said her family had to leave early to get the children home and to bed, Mike was driving the family home from the Ramírez home at nine.

"What did you think?" his mother said. He tried to read her expression but she'd turned toward the window.

Had she noticed that he and Dr. Ramírez—he could *never* call her Ana—had been talking? Of course she had. She'd planned that. Had she noticed how abruptly he'd moved away from the swing to stand and talk with Tim, Luz and Quique? Yes, she saw that, also. She probably thought it showed a strong attraction between him and Dr. Ramírez. Again, she was right, but nothing was going to come of it no matter what his mother's creative brain came up with. He didn't have the time, money or resiliency for a relationship. He might consider that once his family was taken care of.

"Nice family." Mike turned onto I-35.

"That Luz is great." Tim spoke from the backseat. "Did you know she's going into the army in a few months? She's got her whole life mapped out."

"What's she going to do?" Mom put her hand on the back of her seat and turned to watch her younger son.

"After she gets out, she wants to be an architect."

In the rearview mirror, Mike saw Tim shake his head as if in wonder. Tim had never been drawn to smart girls with plans for the future.

"Are you interested in her?" Mike asked to get the spotlight off himself.

"No," Tim denied strongly. "She's way too focused on her future, but she said she'll get out of the army with enough money for college." Tim paused. "Maybe I should do that."

"If you want to go to college, you don't have to join the army," Mike said. "The state pays for college for foster kids. I wouldn't have made it through without that."

Tim shrugged, which meant the end of the conversation. From now on, Mike would leave any vocational considerations up to Luz. Tim accepted ideas from a pretty young woman better than advice from an older brother. No surprise about that.

When he'd parked the car and all three had entered the house, his mother took Mike's arm in the dark living room before he could follow Tim to their bedroom. "Did you like Antonio?" she asked softly.

"He seemed very nice." He smiled down at his mother. "And quite interested in you."

The hand on his arm relaxed. "What did Tim think about him?" he asked.

"Oh." She waved her hand. "I didn't ask Tim. He likes everyone." With a kiss on his cheek, she switched on a light in the kitchen.

What did that say about Mike? That he didn't get along with everyone?

He saw the glow of the hall light. "Are you going to bed?" she asked from there.

"In a minute."

He'd always thought he got along with people, but as he watched her go into the kitchen, Mike had to recognize that since the breakup with Cynthia and with the addition of other responsibilities, he *had* changed, reverted to earlier behavior, silent and closed up. Not that he'd ever had the happy-go-lucky attitude Tim had. If he had, they wouldn't have a place to live.

Heading toward the bathroom and turning the kitchen and hall lights out behind him, he had to admit that, yes, he'd always been different from Tim. Maybe part of that was because he'd been too hurt by their father's second abandonment after Tim's birth.

For years before Mom was incarcerated, he'd been a pretty happy kid, a lot like Tim. He had changed, become less trusting after Mom went to prison and he'd been shuffled from foster home to foster home. No one wanted or put up long with a sullen teenager.

He thanked God for his cousin Francie's support and encouragement. Without that, he didn't know how he would have ended up. Certainly in prison, probably likely to return.

Mike went into his bedroom where Tim was already snoring in his upper bunk. Mike watched him and wondered why they were so different now.

Most likely because Tim had lived with the Montoyas for eight years. They were a great foster family. They'd truly been Tim's family and kept up with him still.

Mike undressed, entered the bathroom and took a shower. As the water slammed down on him, he remembered the terrible emptiness inside him when his mother had gone to prison and the family had been separated. He'd been too masculine, too embarrassed to mention it. Instead, he pretended he didn't care when it had torn him up inside. So no one would know how he felt, he closed in on himself. He bluffed his way through the concerns of teachers and school counselors, keeping his grades up, playing basketball, looking great on the outside. That was how he'd coped then. That was how he was coping now.

Why had it been so important not to allow anyone to see the inside?

Why was it still so important to keep people out?

After getting out of the shower, drying off and brushing his teeth, he went back to the bedroom.

"G'night, Mike," Tim mumbled when Mike came in.

"'Night," Mike said, but the light snores told him Tim had already fallen asleep.

He got dressed before looking at the clock. Only a little after nine-thirty. He was due at work in an hour, so Mike picked up his anatomy book and lay down to read it after he set the alarm. In spite of an interesting section on the ulna, thoughts from the past still bombarded him.

When he got to college, the first year was hard. He didn't know how to make friends, to build a relationship. Then he began to succeed and the shell had begun to crack bit by bit. It split open when he got to medical school. He'd believed his outer shell had disappeared when he and Cynthia were engaged.

After almost half an hour, Tim turned his light on and hopped from the top bunk. When he came back a few minutes later he had a handful of cookies and a glass of milk. The kid ate even in the middle of the night. Tim finished the snack, put the glass on the floor and got back in bed.

"What do you think about the Ramírez family?" Tim's voice filtered down.

"Seems nice." He shut the book, turned to pull his shoes on then stood to leave the room in the hope he could avoid what he figured would be Tim's next remark.

"Yeah."

Mike thought his brother had dozed off, but as he reached the door Tim said, "Ana's pretty, too. And a doctor. What do you think of her?"

He ignored the question. After grabbing his keys and leaving the house, he got in the car and headed to the hospital.

Yes, Ana, Dr. Ramírez to him no matter what she said, had looked great. Her hair was as long and wavy, as beautiful as he'd imagined. He'd had to clench his fists to keep from touching it, from filling his hand with the mass of dark curls. She was wearing a frilly blouse and seemed very feminine and soft, not a word he'd ever associated with her in the past. Sitting next to her on the swing, he smelled her perfume, something flowery and light, felt her warmth, felt himself being drawn to her. Because he couldn't allow that to happen, he'd leaped to his feet and run.

Pretty bad when the pleasure of sitting next to a beautiful woman frightened him, when it seemed like the worst thing that could happen.

What kind of idiot felt that way? Obviously, he was exactly that kind of idiot.

For a moment, he thought about praying. That's what he'd have done a year ago, even a few months ago, but he didn't. He couldn't figure out what to say to God, what to pray for.

Chapter Seven

Two days later, during the next shift Ana and Mike worked together, she could tell his barriers were up and he'd posted guards on every entrance and tower. When she passed him in the hall, he gave her a polite nod. No more Mr. Let's-Have-a-Chat. If she called for transfer, he'd hurry in, move the gurney and leave without a word. The few times she talked to him, he answered, "Yes, Dr. Ramírez," or "Of course, Dr. Ramírez," or "Right away, Dr. Ramírez."

All of those responses, every one of them, were proper ways for a CA to answer a doctor. Why did they upset her so much?

She hit the roof when she looked down the hall and saw Mike and Mitchelson joking and laughing. Why couldn't Mike do that with her? They'd had a nice time at the family gathering a few days earlier. She thought they'd gotten to know each other, but he was more distant than ever.

That was the reason she lost it when she asked him to check on the trache tubes in OR 3 and, again, he'd answered oh so politely, "Right away, Dr. Ramírez."

"All right, Fuller," she'd said in the voice she'd practiced since med school to be as intimidating as possible.

He stared at her in surprise. The staff of the E.R. looked at her amazed. She didn't care. At least this time he had noticed her, really noticed her, but he only said, "Dr. Ramírez?"

"I need to talk to you. Privately." She turned to the clerk and said, "I'm going to use the empty office on E wing."

She stalked off. Once she got to the door, she looked over her shoulder to make sure Mike was following. He'd better be.

"Okay," she said once they were inside and she'd slammed the door behind them. "What's going on?"

He blinked. "What do you mean, Dr. Ramírez?"

"Why are you behaving this way?"

"What way?"

Now she felt foolish and a little embarrassed. She seldom allowed her temper to take over. Now she was in a mess, acting both unprofessional and resentful. How could she accuse him of being too courteous? "So…so cold?" In an instant she realized her mistake. She'd showed him how vulnerable she was, revealing much more about herself and her feelings than she'd meant to. This man muddled her brain and made her forget how she should behave.

"Dr. Ramírez," he said slowly and with great emphasis on the word *doctor.* "If you have a complaint about my work, please discuss that with me in detail and put a note in my employment record."

"I'm sorry. This is so unprofessional." She dug her hands in the pockets of her lab coat. "But you're really confusing me," she whispered.

She caught a glimpse of uncertainty in his expression before he cleared all emotion from his face. He turned to leave without saying a word.

"I need you to…I don't know." She studied his back but his rigid stance wasn't encouraging. "Just don't be so cold. Everyone's thinking something's going on between us. They believe you're angry with me for some personal reason."

He turned back to her with an eyebrow raised. "They are?" He considered that. "No one's mentioned it to me."

Well, of course not. Only *she* thought he was angry with her for a personal reason.

"I don't understand," she said, "We had such a nice evening together, I thought maybe we'd—" She bit her lip to stop the revealing words. "We have to be professional but you're more than that. You're overly polite, and it drives me nuts."

"Dr. Ramírez." He used the same courteous tone he'd used before. "I have two choices in the way I act around you—cold and professional or…something else."

"Something else?"

"Yes." He searched her face. "Like this." He took her by the shoulders, moved her to the corner, away from the window in the door, and pulled her against him to rub his cheek on hers.

The feel of his breath on her neck, the warmth of his embrace filled her with longing and almost made her toes curl up. Confused, she looked up into his face. "What do you mean?"

"If I allowed myself to do what I want to do, I'd kiss you, now."

That sounded terrific.

Ana wound her arms behind his neck. His nearness and his scent—a mixture of man, musky aftershave and disinfectant—jolted her both physically and mentally. She should pull away but was completely thrown off balance by Mike's closeness and, when she glanced up at him, the need in his eyes. She refused to give it up, to shorten the time of this amazing connection.

When at last Mike stepped away, he rubbed his index finger down her cheek. "Dr. Ramírez," he spoke softly but firmly, "your choices for my behavior around you are cold and polite or what just happened between us. I don't know how we could handle this attraction without people starting to talk."

She yearned to return to the circle of his arms but he'd crossed them firmly on his chest. She shook her head in an effort to kick-start her brain, to understand what had happened.

What had happened was that Mike had embraced her, and she'd folded herself in his arms with great delight and enthusiasm. "Could we ignore this? Could we go back to working together in a friendly way?"

He ignored that suggestion. "Coldness or this." He waved his hand as if to encompass what had just happened in this office. When he looked at her, she saw the same confusion she felt. "I've already passed friendship."

"I prefer the second choice." She blinked. "Very much, but you're right. This." She waved her hand around the office as she spoke. "This isn't the best way to act in the hospital or for either of us professionally."

The focus that had guided her for twenty years came back to clear her head. Being found in the embrace of another staff member in a hidden corner of an unused office was not how she wanted to be remembered, was not what she'd worked for all these years.

And yet, how could she forget that moment? Maybe whatever was between them might be better than what she'd prepared for all her life.

She took a step closer and rubbed her fingers along the stubble on his cheeks. When she paused, he moved her hand to his lips, kissed the palm and held it.

With a sigh of resignation, she tugged her hand away. "You're right. As wonderful as this was, it can't happen again."

He nodded, attempting to look cool and distant. It didn't work. The tautness of his expression told her the attraction between the two of them bothered him as much as it did her and that he had made the same decision.

"Let's go back to how we were before—staff members, people who work together," she said.

He nodded again. "Yes, Dr. Ramírez."

"Fuller." The voice of Olivia, the RN on duty, filtered through the thick door. "Transfer."

Ignoring the voice for a second, he kept his eyes on her.

"Fuller, we've got a lot of patients backed up out here. We need you. Now!" Olivia shouted.

Without a word, he strode toward the door, opened it and left the room.

Ana moved to look in the mirror. Light whisker burns colored her neck and right cheek. That was going to be hard to hide and harder still to explain. Her makeup bag was in her locker, but she did have the small tube of lotion she carried in her pocket to keep her hands soft after so many washings. She took it out, squirted a bead into the palm Mike had so recently touched and rubbed it on her reddened skin. That would have to do.

"Dr. Ramírez?" Olivia's voice came from the open door.

"Yes?" She turned.

"I'm sorry I bothered you and Fuller."

What? Did the entire E.R. know what had happened between them? How embarrassing. There hadn't been time for him to tell anyone. Also, she was sure he wouldn't have, so how did Olivia know? Had she been able to see them in the corner? She glanced in that direction.

"I think Fuller is a great CA," Olivia said. "But if you had to call him down, I'm sorry I interrupted. I wouldn't have if we didn't have an emergency."

"No, that's not what I had to talk to him about." Not that she was about to say what the topic had been.

"I know how much you hate to counsel employees on behavior." Olivia nodded sympathetically. "I hope you got your business finished."

"It wasn't—" She stopped midsentence. "Yes, we completed our business." Remembering their business, she grinned. Very inappropriate.

Olivia stepped back into the hall. "You're needed in Trauma 3. Possible broken back from a swimming accident."

"Thanks, Olivia. What are the vitals?" She hurried out of the office and toward the trauma room.

She'd figure out some way Mike wouldn't take the fall for their disappearance, but not now. At the moment, she had a patient and she'd better focus on that, not the touch of that gorgeous but elusive man.

Besides, after a few hours of the rush and stress of emergency room life, maybe everyone would forget about the incident. Almost everyone, but not her and, she felt certain, not Mike.

* * *

What had he been thinking? Mike pushed a gurney into the elevator. Obviously, he hadn't been thinking at all.

An orderly didn't go around holding head residents during working hours, no matter how much the head resident had liked it. There could *not* be anything between them. He was in no position, either financially or mentally, to consider having a relationship with anyone.

Maybe when he finished medical school, they could pursue this.

Oh, sure. *If* he finished med school. By then she'd be married and have a couple of kids.

Why couldn't he get it through his head that a man who'd quit school and was trying to support his mother and brother wasn't exactly a prize? Better to treat Dr. Ramírez with the respect and courtesy she deserved, to pretend he'd never held her against him, that she hadn't leaned into his arms. He had to remember where he was in his life. On top of the emotional turmoil the incident had awakened, he needed this job too much to behave unprofessionally.

How much he needed the job was reinforced when he leafed through the mail on the kitchen table a week later. The electric bill was higher than he'd budgeted. In the credit card statement, he found a charge no one had told him about. Where would he find an extra ninety-eight dollars to cover it?

"I bought some delicious Canadian bacon for you." His mother put a plate on the table in front of him and he began to eat. "It was a little expensive, but I know how much you loved it when you were little." She sat next to him and sipped her coffee. "And I found some wonderful fresh orange juice at the grocery store. I had to get that for your breakfast."

"Mom." He put down his fork. "Thanks for thinking about me. I appreciate it."

"You're welcome, Mike. You take such good care of Tim and me. I want to spoil you a little."

"But we don't have money for extras like freshly squeezed orange juice."

"Oh, dear, but it's not all that expensive. Only about a dollar more a bottle."

"We don't have that extra dollar. I don't know how we're going to pay the credit card bill."

"I had to buy a pair of jeans and some shirts for Tim." She bit her lip. "His were in such bad shape."

"I know, but you need to tell me so I can plan to work more shifts."

"Oh." She nodded. "I promise."

He took a drink of the delicious freshly squeezed orange juice that was worth every penny it had cost. He might as well drink it since they had it. "How's the job hunt going?"

"Not well. Not at all well. I've found nothing since I helped Antonio for a week." She shook her head. "Too bad he doesn't need me anymore, although I'm delighted he's feeling so strong." She sighed. "Employers are so closed-minded about ex-cons, Mike. Almost no one will give me a chance."

He glanced up from his breakfast. "You said *almost* no one. Were there any who would hire you?"

"Yes, but I don't think I would enjoy doing the kind of work they wanted." She fluttered her hands.

"What were they?"

"One was working in a cleaners." She counted off on her fingers. "That would be such hot work. I did that for a year in prison, and it's not pleasant. Another was working in a fast-food place like Tim. I'm his mother. I should have a better job than my son has. One was in a restaurant, washing dishes, I believe."

"I hope you can find a job you'll enjoy, but right now, I need you to get a job. Any job. We need more money and you have to consider your parole status."

She frowned. "Darling, I didn't realize we were in such dire straits."

"Until I got these bills, I thought we were doing better. I haven't had to take money out of the savings account until now."

"I guess I could take one of those jobs."

"Mom, we're going to run out of money soon. After I pay the rent, we might not have enough for other necessities."

"Why didn't you tell me before?" She reached out to pat his hand. "When you don't communicate, no one knows what you want. I'll take the next job I find, even if it's cleaning out a horse stable."

The vision of his mother mucking out a stall in one of her long, spangled dresses and her jingling bracelets made him smile. "Thanks, Mom. You should be able to find something better than that."

"And I'll talk to Tim about what he's doing with the money he's earning. More of that should go into household expenses."

"Great. Tim gets upset when I tell him that. He says it's his money, and I can't tell him what to do because I'm not his father."

"Tim doesn't behave like an adult sometimes."

"No, he doesn't. I bet you can get him to put some in the pot and to buy his own clothes."

"I'll talk to him." She patted Mike's hand. "If

you wouldn't hold everything inside, life wouldn't be so hard for you."

As if he didn't know that already, but the habit of a lifetime was hard to break.

When she stood and waved her hand, her bracelets clinked together. "I'll get the want ads and make some phone calls now." She'd almost reached the arch to the living room when she turned back. "By the way, I've invited Antonio and his family to dinner Thursday."

Antonio and his family to dinner Thursday? Where would he find money to buy food to feed that many people?

"Tim said he'll help buy groceries. Antonio's going to bring the meat so I only have to provide the rest."

That helped on the cost.

She looked at him and bit her lip. "I'd really like you to be here."

Which brought up the more important question: where could he hide from Dr. Ramírez? After what happened in the empty office, the idea of seeing her outside of the hospital, probably dressed like a normal person and with her beautiful hair down, filled him with panic. He opened his mouth to say he was working the afternoon shift when his mother cut him off.

"Don't try to get out of it. I checked your schedule. You don't go in until eleven that night."

"Okay, I'll be here." In a real party mood, he added to himself.

She put her hands on her hips and glared at him. "I don't know why you don't want to flirt with that darling Ana. You seem to ignore her, and she's such a pretty, smart young woman."

"I'll be nice to everyone, Mother," he said. "I always am."

But he was *not* going to flirt with that darling Ana no matter how much she begged.

"Thank you, dear."

Trapped again.

Chapter Eight

Before the guests arrived Thursday evening, Mom said, "Why won't you take the money when it's offered to you? You know Brandon can afford it." She shook her head before she dashed off to wipe the counters again and check on the food in the oven.

Mike looked up from the kitchen table where he was studying an anatomy text book. "I know Brandon can afford it. I know he wants to help Francie's family, but I want to do this myself."

"Stubborn," she mumbled.

"Yeah, it runs in the family." The scent of garlic bread filled the room and made it hard for him to concentrate. He closed the book.

"You and Francie have always been so close.

You know she wants you to take the money and go back to med school."

"Mom, it's because I *do* owe Francie so much that I can't take the money. I owe her everything, but I want to do this on my own."

"That makes no sense at all."

"It does to me. I can't take more from her even if it's Brandon's money. I have to take responsibility for my life, and this is one way I can. This is a start."

"Well, you're going to have to explain that to Francie because I can't." His mother put the teakettle on the burner and leaned over to pick up a dust bunny on the floor, her silver bracelets and earrings swinging with the motion. When she turned to toss the offending particle in the trash, her scarlet dress swung with her.

"She'll understand."

What *he* understood was why Mom had invited Brandon and Francie to the dinner tonight. She'd said it was because she wanted them to meet Antonio. Mike figured that was one reason. The other was in the hope Francie could convince him to take the money.

"You know, even with help, I'd have to work at least forty hours a week to rent the house and buy food. I couldn't do that and go to medical school."

And, yes, he could take out a loan, but with his future looking so dim, he hated to owe more money than he already did from the first year of med school. He stood and headed out of the kitchen, the anatomy book in his hand, then dropped it on the sofa. "Looks like you need to get the table ready for the party tonight. I'll set the table, then I'll study in the living room."

"That's another thing," she said as he took the plates from the cupboard and placed them in a stack on the table. "Why are you studying if you aren't going back to school?"

"Because I like it, because I can use it at work. It's exciting to see what I'm reading about happening right there in the E.R."

But she wasn't listening. The Ramírez family would be here in a few hours and that's what she was concentrating on. The house looked good because she'd forced Tim, who'd complained every minute, to pick up his stuff. Now she was brewing tea and checking the vegetable casserole and a dozen other little chores while he placed a pile of napkins next to the plates.

He was glad his mother was so happy, but Mike dreaded the evening. Being with Dr. Ramírez—because that was what he had to call her in his mind to keep his distance—outside the E.R. made his life complicated and uncomfortable. How could he keep his distance with his mother shoving them together? How could he resist Dr. Ramírez when she had her hair down, wore civilian clothes and smiled? No man could.

At a few minutes after six, Raúl, Luz and Mr. Ramírez knocked. Hearing Mike's shout of, "Come in," they entered the house. Raúl carried a large glass casserole dish while his sister Luz closed the door behind them.

"We're here, Tessie," Mr. Ramírez said.

Mom turned her cheek for a kiss. She glowed with happiness.

"Ana's parking her car. She'll be right in."

"My niece Francie and her husband, Brandon, will be here in a few minutes, too. You'll like them. Plus, she's bringing a wonderful dessert, something chocolate and filled with whipped cream."

"It sounds delicious," Dr. Ramírez said as she entered.

As she entered, Ana glanced at Mike. As usual, he looked terrific. He sat on the sofa, a book in his hands, pretending he hadn't seen her come in. But she'd seen his eyes lift toward her for a nanosecond before he'd begun to read again.

Tonight he wore khaki slacks with a gold shirt

that fit his shoulders marvelously and probably made his eyes look great, which she couldn't see because he'd buried them in his book. Probably the nice clothes meant no pickup basketball game with the neighborhood kids this evening.

"Papi made his wonderful brisket," she said to Mrs. Fuller.

"Brisket? I didn't realize that was a Mexican dish."

"We don't always eat tacos, *querida*." Papi's eyes crinkled in amusement. "Sometimes we eat hamburgers and hot dogs, although we prefer them with hot sauce."

"We have an uncle that carries his hot sauce with him," Raúl said. "Uses it even on chicken tetrazzini, but the rest of us eat almost anything, sometimes without salsa."

"Especially this one." Papi waved toward his son.

"Let's put your lovely brisket in the oven to keep it warm." She walked through the arch into the living room, and the Ramírez family followed her, chatting with each other.

After she entered the kitchen, Ana stopped and looked around her at the art on the walls. She was so engrossed, she barely noticed Raúl place the meat on the butcher-block counter.

A Degas ballerina painted on the wall framed the

table, her long right leg stretched across the corner, "This is beautiful. Was it here when you moved in?"

"I told you about Mom, didn't I?" Mike spoke from only a few inches behind her, so close his breath tickled her neck.

When had he put down his book and come in the kitchen? She didn't care. He was here, and he was close. Very nice. She looked at him over her shoulder. "Art forgery?" she whispered. His proximity made her fluttery and a little breathless. The feeling was so unlike her, she wanted to move away from his warmth but with Luz, Papi and Mrs. Fuller sharing the tiny space, she couldn't move. Unless she shoved hard, like a tackle through the offensive line, she was stuck close to him.

He nodded and took a step back. The movement should have been a relief to Ana but didn't turn out that way. Perversely, she missed his warmth and longed to step back with him.

Mike's mother stood in the middle of the kitchen with everyone studying the beautiful artwork. She looked worried about their opinions, wiping her hands on a towel she'd picked up and trying to read their faces.

"Tessie," Ana said as she slid between Luz and Papi to stand in front of the mural and feel the power of the art, "this is one of the most beautiful paintings I've ever seen. It's absolutely marvelous." She reached out to touch it. "The color, the texture, the use of light, all are amazing."

Tessie stopped twisting the towel, relaxed and smiled.

"*Querida,* I knew about your painting but had no idea how very talented you are," Papi said.

"Let me take you into the hall and her bedroom," Mike said. "You aren't going to believe these paintings, either."

And they couldn't. After many "oohs" and "aahs," several soft strokes across the colors and textures, they returned to the kitchen, overwhelmed.

"These are all lovely." Papi kissed Tessie's cheek. "I'm proud to know a woman with the ability to bring such joy into the world."

She blushed. "Oh, Antonio."

Ana watched her father in amazement. Around Tessie, he was different. She slanted a glance at Mike to see if he was as amazed and amused as she at the relationship between their parents. He didn't seem to have a problem with it at all. Did she? She'd thought she would. With his mother's criminal record, she hadn't been too excited about Tessie, but she made his father happy. He hadn't smiled for such a long time, but he did around Tessie.

Was Tessie a widow? What had happened to

his father? From the way they never talked about him, he must have been gone or dead for a long time. What had Mike done when his mother was in prison if his father was gone?

None of your business, Miss Nosy, she lectured herself.

"I brought dinner," Quique called from the living room. He entered the kitchen and dropped a bag of chips on the table.

"Thank you, Quique," Tessie said politely.

"Nice thought, *mano.*" Raúl laughed.

"Quique knows only three food groups," Ana said. "Fat, carbs and sugar."

"Hey." Quique held his hand up. "I was being thoughtful. I could have just brought myself, which you would also enjoy greatly."

"You're a perfect guest," Tessie said. "I appreciate the addition. Thank you, again." She opened the sack and poured the chips into a bowl.

"*De nada,*" he said with a bow. "You're very welcome."

When Francie and Brandon arrived a few minutes later, Tessie introduced them. Francie seemed interested to meet Ana, smiled and asked her a few questions. Brandon, who was tall, blond and very handsome, hovered around his pregnant wife.

"Why don't you sit here?" He took his Francie's

hand, led her to the sofa and helped her get settled. "I'll bring you something to drink."

"He spoils me." Francie grinned as she watched her husband go into the kitchen.

After Luz arrived, everyone grabbed a plate and walked around the kitchen table to load them up. They could chose from the tender brisket, Mike's favorite corn pudding, green bean casserole bubbling under onion rings, bread, tortillas, guacamole, biscuits, salad, and more.

Plates filled, they crowded into the living room to eat. When Ana entered, she saw the four younger ones on the floor, legs crossed, chatting and joking. She was too old to sit that way and much to old for their conversation. Tessie and Francie sat on the sofa with a space between them. Thinking if she sat there, she could get to know both women better, Ana headed in that direction. Before she could sit, Francie scooted into the empty space faster than Ana had ever seen a woman that pregnant move.

Ana turned toward the now-empty place on Francie's left.

"That's for Brandon," Mike's cousin said with a sweet smile.

"Okay." Ana turned toward the folding chair next to Tessie.

"That's for your father." Tessie smiled, also.

Very suspicious, all this smiling and scooting. The only other seats were the two folding chairs in the corner. With a sigh, she gave up and took one of those. This reminded her of the time everyone had pushed her and Mike together on the swing at her family's house. Here, the room was so small they wouldn't be isolated, just extremely close together.

Brandon left the kitchen, handed Francie her drink and plate before he went back to get his own. As he did, Papi sat next to Tessie.

Almost last to come into the living room was Mike. He saw the place next to Francie and headed toward it, but his cousin said, "It's for Brandon. Sorry."

"You might as well give up," Ana said. "They want us to sit together."

Mike stiffened and turned toward the only empty chair before he walked across the room to sit next to her.

"Sometimes," he mumbled, "they are so obvious. I'm sorry."

He was embarrassed and had become Mr. Closed-In again. She hated all this prickliness and careful stepping around his ego. Not that it made a difference. No matter how their families pushed them together, no matter how much she'd enjoyed the interlude in the office, she wasn't sure she wanted attention from a man so much like her father—well, like the way her father used to be. If she were looking for a relationship, a man who smiled and shared more seemed like a better choice.

So why was she so pleased he was sitting next to her? She had to stop kidding herself. As much as she'd tried to forget what had happened there, the interlude in the office showed the tantalizing promise of what could develop between them.

"Francie's your cousin?" Ana asked after a few minutes of silence under the watchful eyes of both families.

As she'd expected, he only nodded.

She'd known better than to ask a yes or no question. She made another effort but missed again. "Are you two close?"

"Yes." The monosyllable fell into the sudden silence of the room.

She glared at her father and brothers. Immediately everyone started loud discussions.

"Why?" There, she'd finally gotten to an information question. Would he answer it?

"When Francie's father went to jail, she went to live with our Uncle Lou. When Uncle Lou went to jail, she came to live with us."

She almost dropped her fork at the information but forced herself to respond calmly, "I didn't realize so much of your family has served time."

"Francie's certain there's a faulty gene involved." He smiled at his cousin fondly.

"But you and your brother?"

"Haven't been in jail, though neither of us have been immune to the call of the wild side." His smile vanished and he stared back at his plate as if he'd said something he wished he hadn't. "Francie pretty much kept me on the straight and narrow."

"What happened when your mother went to jail? Did you live with Francie?" He was silent. For a few seconds, she didn't think he was going to answer. Was she getting too close to him?

"No, Tim and I both went to live in foster families. Tim's was great. They still keep up with him, have him over for meals. None of mine were great." Before she could ask more about Mike's foster families he hurried on, "Francie was eighteen and living on her own, but she wasn't settled enough to take us in."

It felt as if he were speaking, adding facts, to keep her away from what he didn't want to talk about. She'd like to ask him more: Where was his father? What had his foster homes been like? But she didn't. Miss Nosy did have some boundaries, even if her family teased her about never recognizing one.

"The brisket is good," he said after a few minutes of silence. "It has an interesting taste, sort of spicy."

"It's my father's special recipe. I think he puts peppers and chili sauce in before he cooks it, but he won't share it with us. Says it goes to the first son."

"Is Robbie the oldest?'

"No, my oldest brother, Martín, lives in Houston. Also there's Hector who lives in San Marcos and Laura who's a lawyer San Antonio. They're all older than I am. You've met the rest of us."

"Big family."

"You should see it when everyone comes home. We're really packed in with all the spouses and kids."

They atc in silence until Tim said in a voice loud enough to stop the other conversations, "I think I'd like to snowboard."

"Oh?" Tessie tilted her head to try to grasp what he was saying. "Have you ever been on a snowboard before?"

"No, but professional snowboarders make a lot of money," he continued. "Endorsements and stuff."

In silence, they all stared at him.

"Umm, Tim." Mike paused and looked at Ana.

"Help me," he whispered. "What can I say to convince him this is a stupid idea?"

"I don't think there are any words to persuade him of that," Ana whispered back.

He nodded and didn't say anything.

"Hey, way cool," Quique said.

"There aren't a lot of snowboarding sites in Texas," Francie said.

"There's not, like, a lot of snow in Texas, period," Raúl added.

"I'd have to go to Colorado." Tim nodded and took another bite of brisket.

"When did you decide this?" Brandon asked.

"Saw it on television, extreme sports. Think I could do it."

By now, everyone was struggling to keep from smiling, but it didn't work. They all started laughing, even Quique and Raúl who were just as likely to go off on such a crazy tangent.

"What?" Tim wailed. "No one ever takes me seriously."

"And you wonder why?" Mike teased his brother.

Ana watched the family chemistry and had to laugh again. It was hard to believe with all the Fuller family had been through, but right now they seemed like any normal family, joking and teasing. A moody Mike looked fine and almost too tempting with his smoldering eyes, but a smiling Mike took her breath away.

Once the room had quieted, Tessie said, "I need your help, everyone. I have to get a job. If you know of any leads, please let me know."

"Tessie." Papi took her hand. "You can always come back to the store."

"Thank you, Antonio, but you don't need me any longer. That would be charity and I want to work, to help Mike support us." She looked back at the room. "So, if anything turns up?"

"We'll let you know," Francie said.

Mike and Ana didn't have a minute alone for most of the evening. Although Tessie suggested they take a walk through the neighborhood, Mike refused. Oh, he refused politely, in a way that didn't hurt his mom's feelings, but, still, it was a refusal and probably the right decision.

After dinner, the two of them ended up washing dishes together, trapped into it when everyone left the kitchen.

By accident, he flipped soap bubbles out of the sink. When they hit her in the face, he looked stricken, realizing what he'd done to the head resident. As a reprisal, she picked up a handful of suds and tossed them on his head, which led, of course, to his slapping the water in the sink, which soaked them both. She squealed when the foam started down her neck.

"What's going on in there?" Quique shouted, followed by low chorus of "shhs" from the others in the living room. "Do I have to come in there?"

That question was followed by whispers of, "No."

"Lot of good your coming in here would do," Ana called back to her brother.

Then she looked into Mike's face. His smile had slipped as he ran his gaze over her wet hair, the drips sliding down her face and neck. Finally, he studied her with eyes dark with longing. Reaching out a finger, he slowly and gently traced a soap bubble that rolled down her neck.

She knew, if they were alone, he would kiss her. For a moment she lost herself in the warmth of his gaze, savoring the attraction that zinged between them. She placed her hand on his arms and leaned toward him, yearning to be closer.

Hearing a movement, she glanced toward the arch to see everyone's eyes, sixteen in all, glued on the scene. She jumped back from Mike. When the families realized she was staring at them, they quickly turned away and began a loud conversation while they returned to their seats.

After he dropped his hand to his side, he looked away from the crowd at the door and finished cleaning up, keeping his eyes firmly fixed on the sink. That done, he shouted to those in the living room, "Is everyone ready for dessert?"

Ana moved toward the fridge to take Francie's concoction out but stepped into a small splash of water left over from their horseplay. Her foot slipped from under her, and a searing pain ripped through her right thigh. Biting her lip to cut off the scream, she reached toward Mike as she crumpled. He grabbed her and wrapped his arms around her to keep her upright before she could hit the floor.

"What happened? Did you break something?" He held her tense body against him as she balanced on her left leg.

"It's her thigh." Papi ran to his daughter. "An old injury." He took Ana's left arm. "Help me get her to a chair."

Once she was seated, Ana leaned back and forced her body to relax in an effort to relieve the pain. Deep breaths usually helped. She was aware Mike had pulled a chair next to her and had put his arm around her shoulders, but she ignored his closeness and massaged the muscles to alleviate the throbbing.

"Do you want a cold pack?" Mike whispered.

She nodded, and he went to the refrigerator.

While she rubbed her thigh, she heard the expressions of worry around her and the start of her father's explanation.

"When Ana was about five," Papi told everyone gathered in the kitchen, "my oldest son Martín was helping me paint the house. Ana wanted to help. No matter how many times I told her, 'No,' she kept asking."

"You know what she's like," Raúl said. "Once she decides on something, she doesn't give up."

Everyone murmured agreement.

"What's wrong with that?" she asked through gritted teeth. She took the cold pack from Mike and laid it carefully on her throbbing thigh.

As if he hadn't heard the question, her father continued. "When Martín and I went into the house for a drink, she got a paintbrush and climbed the ladder. I should have known she would. I should have put the ladder away."

Ana heard the guilt in her father's voice. "Papi, you can't blame yourself. It was all my fault," she said as the pain lessened.

"When she got to the roof," Papi said, "the ladder tipped and she fell, all the way to the ground and onto a storm window we'd taken off."

"Oh, no," Tessie whispered. "What happened?"

"The glass broke and shards tore up the

muscles and a lot of other stuff in her thigh. The doctors thought she'd never be able to use that leg again. Even then, Ana refused to give up. She exercised, did physical therapy four times a day, suffered a lot to be able to use the leg."

"But when she twists it, it hurts." Raúl put his hand on his sister's shoulder. "She's the toughest, most tenacious person I know. Nothing stops her from getting what she wants, except that leg."

"But I don't let that happen," Ana said.

"Let's go back to the living room," Francie pulled on Brandon's hand. "It can't be fun for Ana to have everyone watching her."

They left her alone with Mike again. He still had his arm around her shoulder. Now, as the pain began to diminish, she could enjoy his comforting closeness.

"I remember once when I first started work you were in the break room rubbing your thigh." He began moving his fingers up and down her neck in a gentle caress.

"Sometimes if I move awkwardly or stand too long, it begins to ache, but this is the worst it's felt in a long time." She shook her head. "I'm sorry I ruined the party."

"Don't worry." He leaned closer and rubbed his cheek against her hair.

Had he placed a light kiss there, against her curls? She couldn't tell because it happened so quickly, but the thought he might have warmed her.

"I'm better." She looked into his face. Upset because of his worried expression, she rubbed her palm across his cheek. "I'll be okay."

"Take care of yourself, Doctor."

The soft tone of his voice and the concern in his eyes filled her with immeasurable joy.

The party broke up immediately. When Mike took her arm to help her off the porch and to her car, Ana protested. "I can walk fine. I'm fine."

"Just give it up, Doctor. I'm going to help you whether you want it or not." Actually it was a great excuse to hold and support her.

In spite of her continued objections, when they reached the car, he opened the door and carefully handed her inside.

"I can do this." She pulled her legs inside and turned in the seat.

"I know." Once she was settled in her car and had the key in the ignition, he waved and walked back inside the house.

That may have been a mistake. Maybe he should have waited outside until everyone left, because Francie waylaid him immediately.

"What about the money for school?" she asked.

"Thanks, but I can't accept it. I have to take responsibility for my life and my future."

With a sigh, she nodded. "I knew you wouldn't take it, but I want you to know the offer's always open."

"I know." He hugged her.

Francie squeezed him back then whispered, "Ana's better for you than Cynthia. I really like her. Smart, pretty, nice and just right for you."

"Why does everyone assume Dr. Ramírez and I should be together?" he muttered.

"Because you *are,* silly. We all know that. You two just haven't admitted it yet."

He hoped she was wrong—and that she was right. "I don't have time for anything else in my life, not now."

"Love never comes at the most convenient time." She looked out the open front door at her husband, who waited on the porch for her. "Who could have believed a parolee would fall in love with her parole officer? Or that he'd love her—that's me—too?"

"But you're special."

"Mike, you're special, too." She kissed him on the cheek then turned to leave.

With the guests gone, Mike headed back to the

bathroom. Before he got there, he saw his mother on the sofa, her hand over her eyes.

"What's the matter, Mom?" He fell into the seat next to her.

"Oh." She started and glanced up at him. "How's Ana going to be? I hated to see her in so much pain."

"Fine. She says she knows how to handle this." Mike waited a few seconds as his mother put her hand over her eyes again. "Mom, what's really bothering you? I know it's not Ana."

"It's nothing." But she didn't look up.

"Mom, what is it?"

"Oh, Mike." She looked up at him, blinking back tears. "What if I can't find a job?"

"Mom, you'll find a job. It may take a while, but you'll find one." He patted her shoulder.

"But if I don't, how are you and Tim going to eat? He's still growing. He needs clothes and new shoes, and money to go to a movie every now and then."

"Mom, he's working. He has money to do that. I can work more overtime."

"You know I have to find a job to satisfy the terms of my parole." She sniffed. "I've looked all over. Doors close fast when you're my age, have no skills and a criminal record."

Mike squeezed her.

"They put my name on the list at the Biggy-Mart, but people only get jobs as greeter when one of them dies." She took a tissue and wiped her eyes. "And all the fast-food restaurants have enough kids off for the summer to fill every position." She gulped. "I don't know what I'm going to do."

"You tell your parole officer how hard you've looked for work." He squeezed her hand. "We'll make it. We'll be fine."

She stopped crying and wadded up the tissue. "Maybe I'll have to go back to forging paintings again."

He dropped her hand and sat straight. "What?"

"Dear," she said with a pitiful shrug, "forging is the only skill I have."

"No, Mother, you are not going to go back to forgery. No, no, no!" When she didn't say anything, he added, "Your parole officer isn't going to like that."

"What do I care?" She stretched her arms out, the bangles on her wrists sparkling in the light. "I have to take care of my boys."

"No." Mike took both of her hands and turned her to face him. "Listen to me carefully. You're not going to go back to forging. Do you understand?"

She dropped her hands into her lap and the

bracelets gave a light jingle. "But I have to help you somehow. Forging is the only—"

"I know you think it's the only skill you have, but it isn't true. You're friendly and good-looking. I say that even though you're my mother. You might be able to be a hostess in a restaurant or something."

"I'd like that." She looked down at her finger, at the short but nicely manicured nails. "I don't want to go back to forging, but it's the only job I've ever made money at. My pictures were so lovely."

"Yes, but you're not going to do that. You're not going back to that life." She still didn't respond. "And Mr. Ramírez would miss you."

"Oh." She bit her lip. "That's true. Antonio would miss me if I went back to prison."

"We all would." He spoke slowly. "And he would not like you to return to a life of crime."

"I know."

"Promise me you won't think about this anymore."

"All right." She sighed. "It's so very discouraging not to be able to find a job when we need the money. I guess I fell back into old habits."

"Old, bad habits."

The conversation might have been funny if she hadn't been so serious. Had he convinced her to stay straight?

So here he was, thirty minutes later, without a

shower, driving to work at ten-fifteen, headed toward a job he both loved and hated.

What was happening in that little house? His mother had considered returning to a life of crime. They had deep financial problems and his brother wanted to be a professional snowboarder.

"Oh, God." The words left his mouth to his surprise. A prayer he hadn't planned to say had popped out.

"Oh, God," he repeated. "Where are You when I need You?" He stopped at a light and watched for a sign that God was listening. He didn't know what he expected: A sudden strike of lightning? A small voice? Perhaps a wind or a shimmer of light? He looked for any response, but none appeared. Inside, he didn't experience the assurance of God's presence that used to be such an anchor in his life. "Oh, God," he whispered. "I'm worried about Tim, and my mom's unhappy. I'm working hard to live a good life. We all really need You now." He paused again. "Are You listening?"

Again, no answer came.

He'd gone to God in prayer at his lowest time but had received no reply.

Well, that was it. If God wanted to talk with him, God was going to have to start the conversation.

Grabill Missionary Church Library
P.O. Box 279
13637 State Street
Grabill, IN 46741

Chapter Nine

A typical Friday night in the emergency room—sliding from busy to hectic and headed straight toward chaotic. About 3:00 a.m., staff was pulled from other floors to pitch in.

It had started with fifty guests at a banquet with food poisoning. Ten were admitted.

If that wasn't enough of a mess, fifteen coeds from a college dorm came in suffering from exposure to an unidentified poisonous gas. Follow that with several car wrecks, a Harley accident, a couple of gang shoot-outs, miscellaneous chest pain, appendicitis and other cases Mike could no longer remember, and the staff was exhausted and drawn thin trying to cover it all.

Still the ambulances came. Several were loaded with victims from a bar brawl while those in the waiting room filled that area and spilled onto the sidewalk.

With the shrieks and roars of the ambulances, the shouts of vitals from paramedics, the moans of patients and the urgent questions of the families, the noise level intensified. Mike leaned against a wall outside Trauma 3 for a quick vertical nap, a talent he was perfecting, when another sound grabbed his attention.

"Security," Dr. Ramírez yelled from Trauma 4. Shoving himself away from the wall, Mike ran into the cubicle just after the nurse ran out.

Inside stood a man six inches taller than Mike and a hundred pounds heavier. Worse, he waved a long knife aimlessly around the cubicle.

On the other side of the exam table, her escape route cut off by the man, Dr. Ramírez leaned against the wall of cabinets, her eyes wide and frightened. The man on the trauma bed had blood across the front of his T-shirt. From an earlier event or a wound from the armed guy? With his fingers curled around the railing of the bed, the patient looked terrified.

Fear hit Mike hard, almost paralyzing him until a jolt of adrenaline kicked in. With that, he focused, first glancing at Ana then scrutinizing the room to get an idea of the layout and what was going on.

"I'm gonna kill you, Benton." The guy with the knife kept shaking his head as if trying to clear it while the weapon shook in his hand.

"Security," Mike called. Outside he heard people running around, the sound of panicked voices, but no help came. He moved around the room stealthily, shortening the distance been him and Ana while he tried not to alert the man of his progress.

"Thought you'd get away with taking my girl, huh?" the man bellowed at the patient.

"Leave it alone, Jimmy."

The patient tried to speak calmly. Hard to do with a knife inches from his face Mike guessed. "It's over. Barb doesn't want to see you again. She's afraid of you."

Jimmy growled as his lips became taut and misshapen in a chilling grin. As the big man moved around the bed and swiped the knife through the air, his face got even redder, so bright Mike wondered if he were going to have a stroke.

Mike was only a few feet from Dr. Ramírez when she again shouted, "Security."

Jimmy looked up at her as if he'd forgotten she was there. "Why are you staring, lady?"

He turned toward her, raised his left hand—the one without the knife—and backhanded her hard across the face before Mike could move. By the time Jimmy could raise his fist to punch her again, Mike closed the last steps between them. With more strength than he believed he possessed, he sprang away from the wall and threw himself on the man's back. Once there, he reached over the man's shoulders with both arms, trying to keep his balance and to stop Jimmy before he could hurt Dr. Ramírez again.

"Dear Lord, help us," Mike whispered. He kept his balance with his legs scissored around Jimmy's hips and battled for the weapon as the man twisted and twirled around the room in an effort to dislodge him. He prayed constantly for strength and courage, prayed he could distract Jimmy from Dr. Ramírez and the patient.

"Security." Mike held on with a hammerlock, his left arm around the man's neck.

Dr. Ramírez picked up an emesis basin and struck Jimmy on the arms with it, careful to miss Mike and leaping away from Jimmy's reach. As he fought, Jimmy swung his free hand and smashed into one of the large lights over the trauma bed, breaking the glass and cutting his hand. The crystals showered down on the patient and the floor while blood spouted and flowed down Jimmy's arm.

Mike knew he couldn't hold out much longer

against such a powerful opponent. Dr. Ramírez's efforts and the wound in Jimmy's hand seemed to make him even stronger, more violent, almost as if his anger fed off the battle.

"Get off," Jimmy shouted. He shuffled backward and fell against the wall in an effort to smash Mike against it. Air shot out of Mike's lungs but he held on. He had to. At least he'd distracted Jimmy. At least the man had stopped threatening Dr. Ramírez.

"Get out," Mike shouted to her as Jimmy moved away from the exit.

But she ignored him. Instead she replaced the basin with a crutch and began to punch at Jimmy's body.

Still Mike whispered a prayer with every breath. "Please, God. Please, God."

"Security," she called as she landed a good blow in Jimmy's abdomen. It didn't seem to faze the man.

"Shut up, everyone!" Jimmy brandished the knife and methodically beat his back against the wall, attempting to crush Mike with each slam.

Even as Mike softened the blows by bending his knees and pushing away from the wall with his feet, it felt as if his legs were breaking. He didn't know how long they'd last under the bombardment.

Then Mitchelson, the nurse, silently entered the small space. In a second, he grabbed the trauma bed with the patient on it, unlocked the brakes with his foot and shoved it outside. After that, he returned, moving around the edge of the room to take the crutch from Dr. Ramírez and stand in front of her.

"What's the problem, buddy?" the RN asked in a soothing voice.

"He's angry and high on something, maybe meth," Benton shouted from the hall.

Which explained the man's incredible strength, Mike thought as he pulled himself higher on the man's back.

"His name is Jimmy," Dr. Ramírez picked up another crutch and tried to push around Mitchelson.

"Jimmy, you don't want to hurt anyone here," Mitchelson counseled.

In response, Jimmy attempted to scrape Mike off again while he swung the knife toward Mitchelson.

Just as Mike thought he'd have to let go, three security guards and Williams, the big orderly, hurtled through the open door. Seeing them, Jimmy grabbed the crutch Mitchelson held, swung it and hit one of the guards in the head, knocking him down and out.

"You got his arms?" one of the guards asked Mike.

"Not really." Wasn't the swinging crutch

evidence of that? With his last bit of strength, he reached over Jimmy's shoulders and grabbed the crutch as Mitchelson took hold of the other end.

"Hold on. We'll try to get his legs."

After scuffling for a minute, the two guards, Mike and Mitchelson each had a limb while Williams had knocked the knife to the floor and held one of Jimmy's wrists in each of his beefy hands. A guard cuffed Jimmy, which took a lot of the fight out of him. Security hustled him from the cubicle and toward the outer door while Williams followed. Mike bent his knees and flexed them up and down to relieve the knotted muscles in his legs.

"Cops are here," said a nurse to the medical team. "They'll want to talk to you."

Mike and Dr. Ramírez stood against the cabinets, breathing deeply, her face mottled red and white where the man had hit her. "I was really scared," she said in a shaky voice and swallowed hard. "Really scared."

"You were great." He opened him arms and pulled her into them while she shook. With one hand, he rubbed her back; with the other, he held her close, to keep her safe although the danger was over, but more to assure himself she was alive and pretty much unhurt. The fact that he held Ana, breathing, and thoroughly alive in his arms calmed him. He was not about to let go of her.

"Um, Fuller, I hate to interrupt but he cut you," Mitchelson said. "Better let the doctor examine it."

"He cut me?" Mike asked matter-of-factly as he reluctantly let go of Dr. Ramírez and stared at the blood dripping from a wound in his right arm. "I hadn't noticed."

Immediately Dr. Ramírez became a doctor again. "On the trauma bed, Fuller." She looked around before realizing there was no bed and the room was covered with broken glass while the floor was littered with instruments. The knife shone silver and crimson against the white tile floor.

"Guess this is a crime scene now," Mike said.

"Okay, let's go to Exam 1." She pushed Mike ahead of her. "Mitchelson," she asked, once they were in the new room and Mike was on the trauma bed, "what happened to the patient who was in there before this started?"

"Dr. Patel took him to Trauma 3. He's working on him while the police question him."

"I don't even remember what was wrong with the man." Dr. Ramírez shook her head. "Let's get you taken care of, Fuller."

"The police'll need a statement from us, too." Mitchelson got a suture tray while Dr. Ramírez cleaned the cut.

"Your wound is long but not deep," she said as she examined Mike's arm. "Won't take much to hold it."

By the time Dr. Ramírez had finished cleaning and closing the cut, Dr. Harmon, the Director of Emergency Services, bustled into the cubicle.

"Is everyone all right?" She glanced from the gauze on Mike's arm to the bruise beginning to show around Dr. Ramírez's eye. "Guess not."

"We're okay," Dr. Ramírez said. "Minor injuries. Fuller's arm will heal fine."

Dr. Harmon strode toward Dr. Ramírez and studied the redness and start of swelling on her left cheek. "You're going to have a beautiful shiner there. Better put some ice on it. Olivia," she shouted. "Get an ice pack in here, stat." Then she pulled out a small flashlight to examine Dr. Ramírez's pupils. "They're okay, but go home and get some rest." She pointed a finger toward the door when no one moved. "Everyone, home!"

"I can't." Dr. Ramírez moved away from the counter but had to lean against the trauma bed after her second step.

"Doctor, you are in no condition to care for patients." Dr. Harmon squinted at her. Mike thought she might shake her finger if Dr. Ramírez kept disagreeing with her. "You're unsteady, and you won't be able to see out of that eye in a few hours."

Although she kept her hand on the bed, Dr. Ramírez straightened and lifted her chin. "I'm not used to giving up. I can do this."

"No, Doctor, you cannot. Go home and stay there for a few days. If not for yourself, think of your patients. Remember the damage you could do and the hospital's insurance rates."

"I can't leave, not when we're so busy."

"Yes, you can, Doctor." Her tone of voice became more authoritative. "When your boss tells you to, you'd better do exactly what she says." She turned toward Mitchelson and Mike. "How are the two of you?"

Mike held up his bandaged arm. "Fine. A little cut."

"No injuries." Mitchelson put his arms out to show her.

"All right, you two gentlemen go home, too."

"I can't leave. I need the money," Mike said.

"You'll be paid for two shifts. I'll see to that. Don't forget to go to the business office and fill out the paperwork on worker's comp for an injury caused on the job." She waved them out of the exam room. "Get out, all of you. Just to be safe."

Mike tried to support Dr. Ramírez as she left the trauma room, but she shook his hand off.

"Thanks, but I can do this myself."

"Are you sure?" Although he was worried about her balance, Mike recognized her mood and was careful not to take Dr. Ramírez's arm as they walked down the corridor.

She nodded. Color had returned to her face and she'd stopped shaking and swaying, always a good sign. She held the ice bag Olivia had given her against her eye. "It hurts some, but I'm fine. I'm going to change clothes." She gestured to the lab coat smeared with Mike's blood. "Check in the business office then go home." She put her hand on his arm. "Thank you, Mike. You saved my life."

Sometimes all her determination drove him crazy. He watched her walk down the hallway, ambling more than striding but she didn't put her hand against the wall so he guessed she felt steadier. He would have admired her display of self-sufficiency and grit if the whole experience hadn't been so frightening.

Following instructions from security, Mike gave a statement to the police before he went to the business office to fill out forms. Focusing on the forms and his statement, the easy stuff, kept him from reacting to what had just happened.

When he could no longer hide behind routine, when he had to face the attack and the danger to all of them, anxiety filled him. He relived the moment Jimmy hit Dr. Ramírez, and he'd been powerless to stop it. She could have been killed or badly hurt. So could he or Mitchelson. Considering what a crazy man with a knife could do, they'd been fortunate. More than fortunate. They'd been protected and blessed.

"Thank you, God," he whispered.

He looked down at his watch. Almost 7:00 a.m., time to leave, but he had someplace to go before he went home.

In the chapel, three pews lined each side of an aisle wide enough for wheelchairs. On the walls were beautiful stained-glass windows backlit to show scenes of Jesus healing the blind and lame, welcoming the children, curing the leper. A gold cross dominated a Communion table covered in rich green cloth.

Alone in the chapel, Mike sank into a seat in the last row. Although he'd meant to kneel on the step in the front, his legs had turned so weak he couldn't walk farther. Back here, he sat in silence for a moment, eyes on the cross until the scene in the trauma room forced itself into his thoughts.

Over and over again, he saw Jimmy with the knife, hovering over the patient; Jimmy slapping Dr. Ramírez; and Dr. Ramírez hitting him with the basin and crutch. Didn't she realize the danger she'd been in? He could feel himself, dizzily whirling around the room on Jimmy's back, certain the out-of-control man would crush him then go after the doctor with his knife.

He shook all over as if he were chilling. Grasping his hands in an attempt to regain control, he sucked in huge gulps of air as he repeated, "The Lord is my shepherd," over and over. After what must have been at least ten minutes of those terrifying visions flickering through his brain, the shaking slowed and his breathing became close to normal.

Little by little, he realized he wasn't alone. The chapel was filled by a presence. He could feel the Holy Spirit surrounding him, here to enfold and comfort him, to bring him courage and peace.

"Thank you, God," he whispered, aware he and the Lord were communicating again, at last. What else was there to say? Because he didn't want to break this sense of closeness, he added, "For watching over us all, for keeping us safe." He paused because the last prayer was hard. "Please help Jimmy find his way."

As he meditated, tears began to fall, but he didn't try to stop them. Instead, he reached for the box of tissue at the end of the pew to blot his cheeks while he allowed the tension and fear to flow from him. The disappointments and doubts of the past year poured out with them and he turned them over to God. In that moment of gratitude, he recognized God had always been near. God had listened to him every time, every second.

Twenty minutes later, he said another, "Thank you, God," wiped his face and stood to go, renewed. The few minutes had changed him. At the door, he turned toward the chapel again, hating to leave, then he headed to his locker.

He worried about Dr. Ramírez and Mitchelson and everyone who'd gone through the siege. Although still shaky from the experience, inside he was different. Within he felt strong and at peace, finally. He knew he could get through the next few years as he searched for God's will for his life.

How? He didn't know, but now he would listen.

His arm had started to hurt and he felt completely exhausted. Ready to drive home and crash for the rest of the day, Mike pushed through the doors into the E.R.

"Fuller," one of the morning shift nurses said, "there's a message for a Dr. Fuller on the E.R. bulletin board. Guess that means you." She pointed across the hall.

Why would anyone think he was Dr. Fuller? He took down the pink slip and read it.

"Seems you worked with this kid in the E.R. yesterday and her parents want to thank you." The nurse passed him with her arms full of supplies.

"How do you know?" But he knew how. Privacy was nonexistent in the E.R. He guessed everyone had read the note.

With a groan, he turned toward the elevators. He didn't feel like talking to anyone, not now. He wanted to go home and sleep for two or three days. The delayed reaction to the scene in the trauma room punched him in the stomach and neck and sapped his physical strength.

Maybe he'd go home now and come in to see the kid tomorrow, but returning would mean waking up and getting dressed to drive here. Of course, the kid might be discharged by then. Might as well go now. The parents wanted to thank him. That was nice and seldom happened to an orderly. Shouldn't take too long.

While the elevator ascended, he tried to figure

out which patient this could be. He'd worked a double shift and seen at least three or four children. When the elevator stopped at the third floor, he got out and headed toward room 323.

Once there, he glanced inside. The room was filled with balloons and stuffed animals. In the bed, he saw the little redheaded girl who'd come in the previous evening with asthma. She'd been struggling to breathe but had calmed down when Mike talked to her and gave her the polar bear he'd made from a towel.

Leaning over the bed was the child's mother who'd been so worried yesterday. "Dr. Fuller." She smiled and walked toward him. "I'm Julie Andres. I can't tell you how much my husband and I appreciate your care for Sarah."

"Yes, Dr. Fuller. We were so worried." Mr. Andres rose from the chair next to the bed and walked toward Mike with his hand out. "This was the worst attack Sarah has had. We're glad she stabilized. She's going home after a few more tests."

Mike took the hand Mr. Andres extended. "I'm glad I could help, but I'm not a doctor."

"You aren't?" The parents glanced at each other.

"We were sure you were a pediatrician." Mr. Andres let go of Mike's hand.

"No, I'm a CA, clinical assistant." Mike moved

to the bed and smiled at Sarah who, although surrounded by plush animals, still held the towel bear tightly.

"Thank you," she said. "You were so nice to me."

"How are you feeling?"

She took a breath. "See, I can breathe now."

"And her blood gasses are good," Mrs. Andres said.

"I'm glad I was able to help."

Mrs. Andres caressed her daughter's arm. "You're great with children."

"I agree with my wife about that." Mr. Andres sat again and smiled at Sarah. "Thank you."

Mike patted the child's hand before he went to the door and turned to wave at her. When he left the room, he walked down the hall with an unexpected burst of energy. Heading toward the elevator, he passed a big window on the right, the window to the pediatric playroom. He stopped, took a few steps backward and looked inside.

At a table sat a little girl with an IV in her arm and on oxygen. She looked up and smiled. Close to the back wall, a child—he didn't know if this was a girl or boy because the head was shaved—sat in a wagon, reading and pointing out pictures to a woman. An older boy played with cars on another table while a pale little girl relaxed on a window seat and looked out at the view of the capital rotunda.

Children in pain.

Sick children.

Children he could help.

Children God wanted him to help.

He struggled to grasp this concept. God wanted Mike in pediatrics. The revelation hit him hard. He leaned against a wall and thought about it, filled with that certainty that, of course God wanted him in pediatrics. Why should the knowledge surprise him? God had been telling him that since Mike got here. So had most of the staff in the E.R.

God had been leading him, but Mike had resisted almost every step of the way.

He laughed. He didn't stop until he realized the children were staring at him. With another wave, he walked down the hall, confident *this* was where he belonged. This was his future. If it took him years and even more hard work, if it meant waiting until his mother and brother could support themselves, he knew he'd be here someday as a doctor, as a pediatrician: Michael Robert Fuller, M.D.

God had been speaking to him all along, but he'd been too stupid to hear Him, too filled with pain to pay attention, too angry to acknowledge God's voice and leading.

It seemed that, for him, the hardest part of praying was listening.

Smiling, he pushed away from the wall, dodged around the gurney, and ran toward the elevator. He had to tell Ana what had happened.

Chapter Ten

Mike had to see Ana. Because the scene of her being attacked was still clear in his mind, he needed to touch her, to make sure she was all right. And he had to share with her what had happened in the chapel.

It was only as he left the hospital and headed toward his car that he realized he'd called Dr. Ramírez by her first name. *Ana.* On top of that, he'd decided to share this experience with her before he'd considered telling his mother.

Of course, when Mike tried to find someone he'd attempted to ignore for weeks, he couldn't. Her car was no longer in the parking lot. He had no idea of where her apartment was other than "only a few minutes" from the hospital.

He looked in the telephone directory but she

wasn't listed. No way was he going to ask the E.R. clerk for the phone number or address. In the first place, due to privacy issues, the clerk couldn't give him either one. Besides, Mike didn't want anyone to know he wanted to get in touch with her.

His mother would know how to get Ana's number. Did he want his mother to know he planned to talk to Ana? Didn't matter. If things worked out as Mike hoped, she'd know soon enough and be happy about it. She'd probably believe Ana and Mike were together because she'd maneuvered things so cleverly. If they ever got together.

Then he stopped in the middle of the parking lot, as he was putting the key into the lock on his car. What was all this about him and Ana being together?

Slow down, he told himself. He should not rush into anything. Probably better to go home, sleep for a few hours, take tonight off with pay and decide what to do tomorrow. As much as he'd like to talk to Ana tonight, acting impetuously always got him in trouble. Another family trait.

He unlocked the door, got into the car and started the engine.

If he waited until tomorrow or the next day or next week to talk to Ana, he could spend the time until then rejoicing, knowing God had always heard him and that he had a future, that God was leading him.

Would Ana be part of that? Putting the car in gear, he headed out of the lot and turned left.

What an idiot he was. He had a problem with acting recklessly. Actually, that wasn't the problem. He acted recklessly very well. His problem was in slowing down, thinking things through. He knew that, but his mind kept going full speed into fantasyland. It was way too early to consider Ana's place in his life. He shouldn't even think of Ana's sharing his future. Not yet, but he could feel that impulsiveness attempting to take over again.

And yet the entire experience—from the peril in the trauma room to his prayers in the chapel—had clarified his feelings. He couldn't ignore the fact that Ana or he could have been killed. What was the use of putting life on hold when it could have ended in the flash of a knife?

He didn't have to run to her immediately. He shouldn't. That would probably scare her anyway. If the strength of his feelings frightened him, imagine what a shock this would be to her.

He needed to slow down, rein in his rash nature.

What he *could* do was talk to her, just talk to her, tell her what had happened in the chapel, in

Sarah's hospital room. She'd like to hear that. After all, nothing was going on between them. Nothing. They weren't dating. They worked together and were friends, nothing more than friends, through their families. He had no desire to take it further.

Oh, sure.

The truth was, he really wanted to be with Ana, but right now, his life was too crazy for a relationship. He was in no position to consider marriage.

Marriage? Where in the world had that idea come from? Marriage was not a possibility. What was he thinking? Was he thinking at all? He pulled off the road and into a parking lot to contemplate the situation. His mind and thoughts were going around in circles at a thousand miles an hour, headed for a serious crash if he didn't gain control.

Slowing his brain, he attempted to consider the situation, all that he'd gone through that night, and put it into a reasonable, rational order. First, he knew how hard it would be to talk to Ana as a friend and a colleague after he'd held her in his arms again, after she'd clung to him.

Second, he was aware that his family also got in trouble by not only conning others but themselves. It was important that he *not* lie to himself about Ana. The truth was, no matter how hard he tried to deny or ignore it, he wanted more than friendship.

Trying to be reasonable and not to lie to himself, he wondered if it was impetuous to want to be with a woman he cared about more than he should, a woman who'd been the length of a knife blade away from death.

He didn't think so, but he'd made a lot of poor choices during his life.

He didn't need to call her today. Not really. Today he'd sleep and think about things, and life and priorities. He could wait until the next day to come to a decision.

A good plan but a doomed one.

After he got home, he'd slept from eight in the morning to six that evening when he'd gotten up to make a couple of sandwiches. He was a little stiff from riding Jimmy's back and being banged into the wall, but rest and a soak in the tub would take care of that. No big deal.

While he ate, he kept glancing at the phone, almost calling Ana until he realized that he couldn't call her. He didn't have her number and was not going to call Mr. Ramírez to get it. The best thing to do was to watch a little television with his mother, read and go to bed early.

His determination failed. That impulsiveness again.

"Mr. Ramírez," he said when he called at seven-thirty after holding out for an excruciating ninety minutes. "This is Mike Fuller. Could you please give me Ana's phone number?"

"I could, but she's right here. Do you want to talk to her?"

"Sure." The decision of when to call her had been taken out of his hands, hands which at this moment were a little clammy.

He could hear muffled voices, then Ana said, "Hey, Mike. How are you? Have you recovered from last night?"

She thought he was calling to check on her. That was okay, a good start for the conversation. "I'm fine. My arm doesn't hurt much, but I don't mind not working tonight. How are you?"

"Okay. My eye hurts a little. It looks pretty ugly and will get worse. Maybe it's a good thing I'm not going in. I'd probably scare the patients." She paused. "Mike, thank you for coming into the trauma room. You probably saved the lives of both the patient and me."

"Glad to do it." Mike looked around the living room. On the sofa, his mother was sketching and Tim was flipping through a magazine next to her.

Tim reading on a Saturday evening? No way. The kid was trying to listen to his call.

"I'm taking the phone outside. Give me a minute." Once on the porch, he sat on the front step. "I'd like to see you sometime."

"Okay." Her voice sounded pleased. "We can sympathize about our aches and pains. When?"

"Could I pick you up for breakfast Monday?" Breakfast seemed like a good choice. Not a real date like lunch or dinner. That would work until they decided where they were going, if they discovered anything between them. He knew how he felt. Was she interested in anything beyond comparing injuries?

"Breakfast? Sounds nice. Do you know where I live?"

He took down her address and phone number. "Is eight o'clock okay? That's early on a day off."

"Sounds fine. I can never sleep late. I'll see you then."

After they said goodbye, Mike turned off the cell and walked back into the house. Both his mother and brother glanced at him then back at their sketching and reading without saying a word. He picked up the remote and turned on the television.

"Mike," Tim said. "Are you going to use the car tonight?"

"Nope." He searched for a ball game.

"Could I borrow it? I told Luz and Quique I'd try to get the car and take them to a movie."

Luz, Quique and Tim as friends. That was good. Tim hadn't had a chance to make friends in the neighborhood.

"Sure." Mike tossed him the keys.

"What about you and Ana?" his mother asked as Tim hurried into his room to get ready.

"We're going to have breakfast together on Monday." Before his mother could begin to celebrate, he added, "Only breakfast, Mom. That's all. Don't get excited."

He shouldn't have wasted the warning. His mother tried to hide a smile but he knew she was humming "Here Comes the Bride" inside her head.

"I'm going to church tomorrow morning." Mike sat down and turned on the television to watch the Astros. "I'd like you to come with Tim and me."

"To church?" She stopped humming and gazed at Mike with a blank expression. "Why would I go to church? I mean, really, why would I want to?"

Putting the remote down, Mike said, "Francie took me to worship a couple of years ago. I really liked it. I stopped going for a while, but that was a mistake. Francie took me back to church just a few weeks ago. I've missed it. Church helps me. God gives me strength to live the way I believe I should. I'd like to share that with you."

"Sunday at church?" She glanced at her lap and smoothed the gauzy material of her mauve skirt, her bracelets jingling with each movement. Then she looked at him. He thought he could see terror and sadness in her eyes. "Mike, I'm not good enough to go to church. I'm not one of those churchy-type people."

"Mom, you'll be accepted and loved at this church. Francie goes there. If you're uncomfortable at any time, we'll leave, but I'd like to share this with you."

"I don't know." When he didn't push anymore, she nodded. "All right." She sighed. "If it makes you happy. What time do I need to get up?"

"We'll leave at ten."

She fidgeted a little more. "I dress funny." The panic was back in her eyes. "Not like those churchwomen in their expensive, fashionable clothes and purses and matching high heels. What should I wear?"

"Mom, Francie started going to church there only a few months after she got out of prison. She wore old jeans, but neither her clothes nor her past made any difference with the church members. They'll love you. They want you there. God wants you there and doesn't care what you're wearing."

"Oh." She nodded. "I'll try it once."

"Once," he agreed.

Sunday morning went well. They sat with Tim, a very pregnant Francie and her husband, Brandon. His mother had stayed through the service and had charmed everyone who introduced themselves to her, including the minister.

After the service, his mother agreed that she might try it again. After all, she got to see Francie and Brandon and the songs were pretty, too. The preaching she wasn't as sure about. "The man surely hit a lot of tough places in my life. Felt sort of like meddling to me."

"That's one ugly shiner." Ana studied herself in the mirror. Her eye, surrounded by deep purple bruises, was almost swollen shut. The ice packs she'd used probably helped some, but her face would be a multicolored splendor for days.

What should she do about it? This girlie stuff was as new to her as were all the bruises. Should she cover them? No way. Although she might be able to even out the skin tone, nothing would hide the swelling. And to cover the purple would take more concealer than Wal-Mart carried.

With a sponge, she patted on a little liquid foundation and puffed on a light dusting of powder. That was the best she could do. If she turned her head to the side, she looked okay: khaki slacks, nice makeup, a pink cotton tee that flattered her complexion. Pretty good except for the really ugly part around the other eye, which nothing could help.

She picked up a pair of sunglasses and slid them on. Better. She wouldn't scare people on the street.

But should she wear them in the restaurant? Would it be impolite to sit across from Mike in sunglasses?

"Stop being such a girl," she told her reflection. "This is just breakfast. Nothing big. When did you get to be so wishy-washy? So anxious to please?"

Since she saw Mike the first time, she answered herself.

Whirling away from the mirror, she left the room, grabbed her purse and headed downstairs to meet him. After all, this wasn't a date. No reason he should come up to her apartment when this wasn't a date.

Odd, but she felt as though it was one.

As she was getting off the elevator, she saw Mike standing in front of the other one. How embarrassing it would've been if he'd gone up in one elevator while she'd come down in the other. They could have played that game for hours.

She might as well give up. She'd never been cool and felt fairly certain she never would be.

"Hey." She grabbed his arm. "I decided to meet you down here."

He didn't seem to notice she was uncool. Instead he scrutinized the bruises he could see, then reached out to take off her glasses. He gently touched the corner of her eye.

"How does it feel?"

"Do you want a medical or a personal description?"

"Personal."

Something about his being so close and the gentleness of his touch made it hard for her to speak and think. With a concerted effort, she cleared both her throat and her befuddled brain. Neither effort was completely effective.

"It aches, exactly the way someone like you with a year of medical school would know." She blinked. "I'd be no good in the E.R. because I can't see out of that eye. I have no depth perception."

He handed back her glasses. Then, being careful not to touch the bruised area, he put his palm on her cheek.

"How's your arm?" she asked. Oh, the man was potent. It was hard for her to put a few coherent words together with him watching her and so close.

He rolled up the sleeve on his blue plaid shirt. "Under the bandage, it looks fine. I had good medical care."

"Did you change the dressing?"

"Yes, Doctor. Twice a day as instructed."

She nodded at the same time she realized she'd certainly started their time together off on the wrong foot, more like a medical consult. "I want to thank you again. I was never happier to see anyone than I was to see you."

Holding the door open, Mike allowed her to precede him then moved to the street side of the walk. A gentleman. She slipped her glasses back on.

"There's a diner a few blocks down that has great food. It's an easy walk."

"I've always thought I could do anything I wanted by willing myself to do it." She matched his steps. "But when I saw that man swinging the knife—" she shook her head "—I knew I wasn't going to get out of it alone."

"You were holding your own. If you'd had better weapons you'd have taken him out."

"Possibly, but the emesis basin wasn't doing much damage."

"I've never seen anyone use a crutch as a weapon like a samurai warrior."

"Only not as successful." She shook her head.

The thought made both of them smile. "I didn't think I'd ever find the experience funny," she said. "I guess humor is one way to cope."

As they waited for the light, Ana asked, "What did you want to talk about?"

He didn't answer, just kept walking. She knew his ability to duck a question. Behind those beautiful dark eyes lived a man as uncommunicative as her father.

Thank goodness Mike did have such beautiful dark eyes or she might not put up with that.

"The Best Diner," Ana read the name over the door. "It looks nice." She waved at the big plate glass windows with red-and-white checked curtains.

"It's my favorite place." Once inside, Mike waved at the cook. "Hey, Manny, why are you cooking breakfast? I thought you only did lunch and dinner."

"Morning cook got sick." The man Mike had called Manny wiped his hand on his apron and came out of the kitchen. "Good to see you, kid."

The two men shook hands and hit each other on the shoulder before Mike led Ana to a booth and slid in across from her.

"Who's this lovely young lady?" An attractive dark-haired waitress dropped two menus on the table.

"This is Ana Ramírez. She's a doctor at the hospital." He waved a hand at the two who were studying Ana. "Ana, these are two of my best friends, Julie and Manny Trujillo. They're almost like family."

"What do you mean *almost?*" Julie said. "We are family." She pointed at Mike. "This is the greatest kid in the world. You be nice to him."

Ana smiled. "Yes, ma'am."

"Nice girl," Julie said. "Pretty, too."

"Come on, Julie. Don't embarrass them." Manny waved toward his wife. "She's always butting into other people's business. Ignore her."

"Only for their own good," Julie said. She flipped her order pad open while Manny hurried back to the kitchen.

"Why are you here so early?" Mike asked the waitress.

"When Manny gets up this early, I can't go back to sleep." She pulled out her pencil. "Talked to your cousin Francie yesterday. She said she's taking it easy but doing okay."

"She's doing great." He leaned toward Ana. "My cousin used to work as a waitress here."

"We love her." Julie smiled at Mike. "You want a number four?"

Mike nodded. "The usual."

"Don't even write that down," Manny said from the kitchen. "The kid wants orange juice, two eggs, sunny-side up, bacon and a stack."

"They know you pretty well here." Ana laughed as she studied the menu. "I'd like Fruity Fiber cereal and a cup of coffee. Black."

"That's all?" Mike asked.

"Not everyone can eat like you and not put on weight." Julie handed the order to the cook and brought them water and coffee before she moved to wait on another table.

"Tell me about your name," Mike said. "I know Manny has two. He's Manuel Trujillo Rivera."

"I use my father's last name, Ramírez, and my mother's last name, Gutiérrez. My full name is Ana Dolores Ramírez Gutiérrez." She took a sip of coffee. "We used to put *y* meaning *and* between the names, but no longer."

He nodded and repeated, "Ana Dolores Ramírez Gutiérrez. Very pretty name."

"Thank you. *Muchísimas gracias.*" Ana put her cup down before she asked again, "So, what did you want to talk about?"

He grinned. "You always go right to the problem don't you, Ana?"

She raised a brow but made no comment when he called her Ana. Of course, she'd told him to, but he hadn't before. He seemed to feel more comfortable with the name now. She guessed saving another person's life did that.

"I had a great experience the other night." He drummed his fingers on the table. "I want to tell you about it, but this isn't easy for me to share." He stopped for a few seconds. "After the fight in the E.R., I went to the chapel and prayed."

"I didn't realize you're a religious person." She studied him seriously. Sharing religious experiences had always made her more than a little nervous.

"For a few months I haven't been. I haven't felt the Holy Spirit in my life."

"Oh?" She leaned back and bit her lower lip. "Mike, I'm not comfortable discussing religion."

"I understand. I used to feel that way, too, but I'd like to share what happened."

Sharing was good. She nodded uncertainly.

"I prayed for you, Mitchelson, Williams and everyone in the emergency room."

"Thank you. We can all use that."

"Here's your juice." Julie set the glass down and topped off the coffee cups before she moved away.

"Then I prayed for strength and guidance. For myself." Mike took a drink of the juice. "Francie says her faith changed her life, helped her change. I started going to church with her a couple of years ago." He looked up at the ceiling for a few seconds. "This is hard for me to explain."

"Go on," Ana encouraged. "This conversation makes me feel a little weird, but I know it's important to you."

"Like I said, I used to feel uneasy about discussing another person's faith, too." He paused and took a drink of water. "Okay. Here's what I wanted to talk about."

He still didn't say anything so Ana sipped her juice and waited, as hard as that was for her.

"A few months ago, I went through some hard times. I had to quit med school because my brother and mother came to live with me. I had to work to support us. On top of that, there were some other things going on, too. All that stress and change hurt my faith. I began to believe God wasn't around."

"And now?" She'd begun to find this interesting. Mike's face no longer looked like stone, as if he couldn't communicate. Now his eyes sparkled with excitement, and he spoke with emotion and conviction. He reached over to take her hand. It felt nice in his, warm.

"When I was in the chapel, I knew the Holy Spirit was there," he continued. "I prayed and knew my prayers were heard. It's hard to believe, but it happened. I felt it." When she squeezed his hand, he said, "After I left the chapel, I went up to pediatrics because the parents of a patient wanted to thank me for helping their daughter in the E.R." He shook his head. "They both assumed I was a pediatrician."

When he didn't speak, she said, "What happened after that?"

"I walked down the hallway and saw the children in the pediatric playroom." He held her hand more tightly. "I believe I can help children. I know that's where I belong."

"Okay." She nodded again and waited for him to go on.

"That's it?" he sounded more than a little disappointed when she didn't share his happiness. "I thought you'd be surprised or excited."

"Mike." She looked down at their linked hands. "We all know that pediatrics is where you belong. I've told you that. Everyone in the E.R. has told you that."

He blinked. "Oh, yeah. I forgot, but this time God told me that."

"Yes, and He is higher on the chain of

command. If it took God to knock some sense into you, I'm very happy God took over." She leaned forward. "What does this mean in your life? Will you go back to med school?"

"I haven't worked the details out, but now I have hope. When everything crashed in on me, it was too much. Now I realize eventually Tim will move out, Mom will find a job, and I won't have to support them for the rest of my life."

"Did you really think you'd have to?"

"You've met Tim, right? Didn't that professional snowboarding idea give you some insight into him?"

"Yes, a little. I can see why you'd thought Tim would be around for a while."

"It's more like I'm afraid Tim would never grow up."

"He's always been a little, um, different?"

"Immature."

"Well, then, how did you get so responsible while Tim is immature?"

"Okay, here it is." But he didn't say another word for several seconds. "He's had a rough life. Never knew his father. Dad disappeared after I was born, came back for a year, just long enough for Tim's birth, then left again. When Mom went to prison, we both went into foster care. He drives me nuts sometimes." He fiddled with his napkin. "But I understand why he's the way he is."

"You went through the same things."

"Yeah, and at eighteen, I was pretty messed up, too."

"Is that why you didn't get Tim from foster care?"

"You know, you don't have to push me all the time." He looked into her eyes. "Right now, I'm willing to communicate without your help."

"Sorry." She put her hand over her mouth.

"Anyway, his foster family, the Montoyas, was great. They loved Tim and really helped him. All of us—the social worker, the Montoyas, Tim and I—felt it was better for him to grow up in a strong family because I couldn't take on a twelve-year-old boy with 'attachment issues' then." He shook his head. "I felt guilty about that decision, but I've prayed about it. This was best for Tim."

She bit her lip. "I don't know much about faith and religion, and I really don't understand prayer, but I'm glad you've made the decision to be a pediatrician."

As Ana spoke, Julie placed Ana's breakfast in front of her.

"Thank you," Ana said. "It looks wonderful."

"Hey, this girl is nice." Julie put Mike's breakfast down and scrutinized Ana for a few seconds.

Mike wanted to leap to his feet, grab Julie and hustle her back in the kitchen. He knew what she was fixin' to do. Exactly as Manny had warned, Julie couldn't stay out of other people's lives. Why hadn't he remembered that before he brought Ana here?

"You know," Julie nibbled the end of her pencil, "I like her a lot better than I did Cynthia."

Chapter Eleven

Who was Cynthia?

Ana became even more curious about the identity of this Cynthia when Mike dropped his gaze to the plate piled high with food, picked up a fork and began to eat with great pleasure.

She knew that trick, doing something else when he didn't want to talk and hoping no one would notice. That was a tactic her father used when he didn't want to talk about—well, about anything.

Ana poured milk on her cereal and examined Mike's expression, which showed only enjoyment of his breakfast. "So, who's Cynthia?"

He took another bite and chewed. When he swallowed, he used his fork to pick up another bite of egg.

Putting her hand on his wrist to keep the fork

on the plate and away from his mouth, she repeated, "Who's Cynthia, and why does the mention of her name make you so nervous?"

He looked at her then at his fork.

"I'm not going to stop asking so you might as well answer," she said.

"Sometimes you're very pushy."

"I don't consider it a bad quality. Don't try to change the subject. Who's Cynthia?"

"An old girlfriend."

"What's so bad about that? I'd expect you to have dated lots of women. You're a very good-looking man."

He nodded stiffly. "Thank you."

How cute that he was so uncomfortable. Maybe as attractive as he was, he wasn't the Mr. Cool around women she expected him to be. "Were you serious?"

He started to pick up the syrup but glanced at her, knowing she wouldn't back down. "We were engaged."

"What happened?"

His eyes lifted to her face again before he grabbed the pitcher and poured the syrup over his pancakes. "You're not going to give up?"

Ana shook her head.

"Even if it's personal and I'd rather not talk about it?"

"If it's personal, and you'd rather not talk about it, just say, 'It's personal, and I'd rather not talk about it.'"

As she'd hoped, the whole thing sounded so foolish that he gave up and said, "She broke the engagement when she found out I couldn't get married for a while."

"Because of your mother and brother?"

He nodded. "And because I had to quit med school."

"Julie's right. I am nicer than Cynthia."

The words brought a smile to Mike's lips.

So he'd had to quit med school to support his family and because of that his fiancée had broken up with him. She'd really misjudged him. He wasn't lazy and unmotivated. Just the opposite. Hardworking and determined were very attractive traits to Ana.

After another sip of coffee, she noticed Manny and Julie watching them, whispering and grinning. Why? Those two were acting as if they thought Mike and she were on a date.

She blinked. Were they on a date? She really didn't know. She'd thought Mike had asked her for breakfast to discuss how they felt about surviving their shared experience, the terror they'd gone through together in the E.R. less than forty-eight hours ago. Maybe to debrief, to get better acquainted with each other because the incident had brought them closer.

Perhaps that wasn't the reason.

He *had* brought her to a special place, introduced her to friends, held her hand. He'd shared but been embarrassed about his ex-fiancée whom he'd also brought here and probably held *her* hand, as well.

This breakfast was beginning to feel like a date the longer they sat together, and a quick glance at his face didn't give her any clues. He was enjoying his pancakes. That was all.

She really needed to know. If this *wasn't* a date, she should force herself not to notice how handsome he was or how beautiful his eyes were. But here she was: drooling over his looks, mentally noting his good qualities. She acted as if this were the beginning of, if not a serious relationship, at least some kind of relationship when she had absolutely nothing to go on.

Yes, it was nice he wanted to share the answer to his prayer and the renewal of his faith. As she took a bite of her cereal, he smiled at her. His eyes showed interest in her.

Of course, she wasn't very good at interpreting the message found in the eyes of attractive men. Maybe he was smiling because he'd just finished a mouthful of Manny's pancakes. She didn't know, and she'd better find out before she became too infatuated with him.

A little infatuation she could handle. That was the sort of thing that sent out sparks of happiness and enjoyment and made life more fun, but that wasn't where this train was heading. Her destination looked to be a Big Infatuation. She didn't want to arrive at that junction alone. She wasn't sure she was willing to risk following that track no matter who was on the ride with her.

All of which was far more railroad imagery than anyone needed. Right now, she had to find out the reason for this…um, this meeting.

Date or no date?

"Why are we here, Mike?"

Still chewing, he looked up, surprised. When he swallowed, he said, "Don't you like Manny's cooking? Well, probably not because you're eating cereal, but just try a bite of these pancakes." He cut off a small piece with his fork, dipped it in a little syrup, and held it out. "You're going to love this."

Eating pancakes from Mike's fork seemed a little, um, intimate, but what could she do? It would be rude to allow him to sit there, fork extended and dripping syrup on the table. She leaned across, took the morsel between her lips, chewed and swallowed. He was right.

"That is good."

"Yeah, Manny's a great cook. Francie loves his soup, any kind. I promised I'd get her some next time I was here." He checked the large red clock on the wall. "I wonder if he has anything ready this early."

"Did you eat here a lot when your cousin worked at the diner?"

He nodded. "Yeah, she…um…started working here after she got out of jail. Julie hired her. We've all been grateful for that."

What? "Francie was in jail, too?" She attempted to keep the shock out of her voice.

He nodded again. "Actually, a lot of my family has been, except Tim and me."

She sat back. Why had Francie been in jail? How did she feel about so many members of his family serving time? Surprised, yes, because Mike didn't look or act like someone from a family of criminals. Francie was doing so well now, and his mother was trying hard to make a new life. Her father had told her that. Her father wouldn't be interested in a criminal.

But Tessie had just gotten out of prison. She was a criminal. At least, a former criminal.

"I don't have the best family background, Ana. Francie worked really hard to break us of the family propensity toward crime. I'm determined to make a good life, too, for me and Tim and our mother."

"What was Francie in prison for?"

"I'd…I'd rather not say." The closed-off look fell across his face.

She could understand his reticence. Pushy as she was, she occasionally did understand and recognize limits. "Okay, I do have a question I hope you'll answer," she said, returning to her earlier concern.

He looked at her, uncertainty showing in his expression.

"What is this?" She tapped the table with her index finger.

"You mean your cereal bowl?"

"No, what I mean is…" She hesitated. What had happened to that pushy person who never was embarrassed and *used* to inhabit her body? "Is this a date? What we're doing this morning, is it a date?"

"I think so." His puzzled eyes looked into hers as if trying to read her thoughts. "Isn't it?"

She sighed in relief. "I just wondered. I didn't know if we were friends discussing life or if this were a date."

"Do you mind if it's a date?"

"Not a bit. I just wanted to know." Realizing she wasn't going to eat any more of the cereal that had turned into mush while they talked, she put her spoon down and pushed the bowl away as she leaned forward. "Have you considered the consequences of our dating? There are people at the hospital who will gossip about us. Others will see anything I do for you as the result of our being close, not because you deserve it."

"None of that bothers me, but I didn't stop to consider how you might feel." He smiled. "I was so relieved when you weren't hurt Saturday night and so excited about God's leading, I wanted to see you, to tell you." He reached his hand across the table toward her. "I want to be with you because when you were fighting that guy off..." He paused, shook his head. "After that, after knowing he could have killed any of us, I realized how hard it is to foresee what life will bring."

"That's true."

"After that, I knew I had to see you now, to tell you..." He didn't finish the sentence but studied her face. "I want to be with you. Now. I don't want to put off being with you until I have enough money or I'm a doctor." He took her hand.

Grasping his fingers, she said, "I'd like that, to

be with you." They gazed at each other. She could hear Manny and Julie chattering in the background but ignored them.

After a few minutes of mindless bliss, her expression turned into a frown. "The problem is this religion thing. I didn't grow up in the church. My parents never took us. It's something I've never even thought about for myself. I sleep, work or study on Sunday mornings."

"I used to be that way, but my faith changed that. Oh, I've been off and on, but no more. God's always been there when I listen. After the experience in the chapel, I'm really paying attention to God's way now."

As she scrutinized him, she could see that change. Overnight, the edge was gone. He wasn't as nervous and worried as he'd been when they first met. A feeling of calm and restfulness flowed from him now. "I'm impressed by the difference I see in you, but for me?" She shrugged. "I don't think that's me."

"I'm not going to push you, but I would like you to come to church with me on the Sunday mornings we're not working."

"I don't know if that's really for me. It's not my kind of thing."

"It won't hurt, I promise. We can spend time

together, go to lunch, eat with your family or mine. We can be together." He rubbed the palm of her hand with his thumb. "I won't push, but I'd like to be with you whenever possible, and I'm going to be in church every Sunday I can."

She'd like to spend time with Mike, lots of time, but the idea of going to church tossed up warning signals. In this, she and Mike were different. Although they had lots of things in common, religion wasn't one of them. She'd lived almost thirty years and her father had lived his entire life fine without church.

But she also liked the feel of his hand in hers, his touch against her palm and the look of joy in his eyes.

"All right. I'll try it, but I'm not going back if I don't like it."

"That's all I ask. Try it."

After she put her hand on Mike's, a thought struck her. "Your mother. Does she go to church?"

"She didn't want to. I had to work on her, but she went with Tim and me yesterday and liked it."

Her father's life was about to change, too. It would probably be good for him because he needed to get out more, but for her?

"Maybe we could do some other things besides church. Do you think we could go to a movie sometime? Take a walk? You and your family could come to my apartment for dinner if we'd all fit," she suggested.

He dropped his hand to finish the last of his breakfast. "I don't have much money so we have to do inexpensive things, but I want to see you, spend time with you. Maybe we can go to some of the free events at Zilker."

For the next minute, the silence was filled with the comfortable sounds of Mike dragging his final bites of pancakes through the syrup and eating them.

"You need another stack?" Manny shouted from the kitchen.

"No, I'm finished." He held his empty plate toward Julie, who picked it up and cleared the table. "But I'd like some of Manny's good vegetable soup for Francie."

"I'll get it for you." Julie turned and carried the dishes into the kitchen.

"What about the check?" Mike said.

"We'll put it on your tab." Manny smiled and waved from the kitchen.

"Which means they won't accept my money." Mike shook his head. "I love these people and would like to eat here more often, but I wish they'd let me pay."

"They love you. Accept it."

"I should." As he stood and reached his hand out to help Ana slide from the booth, Julie put a carton down on the table.

"There's Francie's soup." She grabbed Mike in another embrace. "Give her a hug from us."

"How's your Mom's job hunt coming?" Ana asked after they left the restaurant and ambled toward her apartment. "Has she found anything?"

He stuffed his hands in his trouser pockets. "No. She doesn't like what's available but has agreed to consider any job. Her parole officer is getting concerned, although he's happy she's still looking."

"I'll check around, talk to some friends. Maybe there's something at the hospital."

"With her past? The conviction and prison time?" He held the front door of the building open for her. "Would they hire her?"

"The conviction wasn't for violent crime or drugs, right?" When he nodded, she said, "If it had been, there wouldn't be a chance. I'll look into it."

"I'd appreciate it." He shook his head. "I hate to ask you to do this."

"You didn't. I like your mother." She smiled at him. "And my father likes your mother."

Once inside the lobby, Ana pushed the elevator button. "Thanks for breakfast." She touched the puffy bruised area around her eye. "I'm going back to work Wednesday morning. Guess I'll see you on the late shift."

"I'm walking you to your apartment."

The elevator door opened.

"You don't have to."

"I know. I'm going to anyway."

When they got off on the third floor, she pulled the key from her purse and put it in the door. "Thank you again," she turned to say.

Setting down the bag with the soup in it, Mike reached out and put his arm around her shoulders to pull her into an embrace. He held her for a few seconds, his cheek resting against her hair. Then, with a smile, he stepped back, picked up the soup and turned toward the elevator.

Nice, very nice. Ana watched him go before she unlocked the door and went inside.

He hadn't kissed her. Probably too soon for that but she knew he liked her, liked her enough to take her on a date to a diner to meet friends, liked her enough to cuddle for an instant in the hallway.

All in all, with the exception of learning about his religious faith, this had been a great morning. She should be grateful. His faith had made him more open and willing to share with her. He'd spoken about something important to him, a breakthrough for Mr. Stone-face. It might mean they had a future, if he were willing to keep communicating.

Idiot! She was acting like a love-struck teenager with a big crush on the quarterback of the football team. No matter how smart and handsome Mike was, there were problems between them, a whole lot of problems.

A chasm separated Mike's relatives from her law-abiding family, although her father was attempting to bridge that. Her worry that Mike had been lazy had disappeared when she discovered everything he was coping with. She wondered if that Cynthia hadn't caused real damage when she broke up with Mike. What had that done to his self-esteem and ability to trust?

In addition to those family differences, the rigid hospital hierarchy made a relationship between a doctor and an orderly difficult. And there was that religion thing. This morning, they'd addressed a few of these issues. With further communication, they could probably handle anything that stood between them.

Did she really believe that or was she allowing his gorgeous eyes and beautiful smile to convince her?

"Hey." That afternoon, Tim sat next to Mike on the couch and shook his older brother to wake him up.

"Yeah?" Mike stretched and yawned. He must've fallen asleep watching baseball, a great sport to nap through.

"Did I wake you up?"

Mike stifled a sarcastic response. "What do you want?"

"Well, the other day I talked to Luz about the army. I think I'm going to join."

"Terrific." Mike sat up and swung his feet to the floor. "I really think it's a good idea, but you know you don't have to if you want funds for college."

He nodded. "I know the state will help me, but, you know, I'm a little immature."

Mike again bit back another insult. Instead, he nodded and said, "We all are, from time to time."

"Yeah, but with me it's sort of a lifestyle." Tim stared at his hands before he looked at his brother. "You've always taken the load in this family. Mom tells me you're having trouble with the bills."

"You've been putting in money. That's helped."

"But I'm not going to make much if I stay at the restaurant. If I go into the service, you won't have to feed me, and I can send some money home."

This was getting emotionally deep again, but it was one conversation he couldn't run from. "Tim, you don't have to move away. If you want to stay in Austin, we'll handle the finances somehow."

Tim nodded.

"Don't go into the army unless you want to. It's a long commitment."

"I'm ready for it. I really think I am." Then Tim stood quickly, patted his brother on the shoulder, said, "You're a great brother," and hurried out of the room.

Mike smiled. They were more alike than he'd thought, both hating to show emotion, hating to express or be part of it. Kind of a male-Fuller thing.

Chapter Twelve

On Friday evening almost two weeks later, the break room was packed with staff members who'd headed there to sample the Texas pecan cake Olivia made for Mitchelson's birthday.

Mike caught a glimpse of Ana across the room. During those weeks, they'd gone out a few times since the breakfast at the diner. Late one evening, he'd taken her for a hamburger before they both worked the late shift. He'd rented a movie and they'd watched it with Tim and Quique. Once they played miniature golf and often grabbed a sandwich together during their dinner breaks.

He smiled at the memories. Now, as the staff gathered, he watched her pick up a candied cherry from her napkin and pop it in her mouth. She grinned when she noticed his scrutiny.

"One of the patients today said this hospital sure could use some brightening up," Olivia said as she cut herself a piece of cake. "What do y'all think?"

"My first day here, I was surprised how gloomy it looked," a new orderly said.

"And the floors are gray," Ana agreed. "It's depressing. I know we work in a hospital, but does it have to look like a hospital?"

"Every room should be bright, should make people feel better." Mike licked a smear of the sticky glaze from his fingers.

"Didn't I hear once that the hospital was going to have an artist do some paintings after the renovation?" Ana nibbled on another cherry.

"I heard that, too," Olivia said. "But I haven't seen any paintings."

"Murals. I think they were supposed to be murals," the respiratory therapist added.

"Well, I sure would like something cheerful in the waiting room," Maybelle, the receptionist said. "It would make my job a lot easier if it cooled some of those patients off."

Mike watched Ana savor the cake. He liked her enjoyment of the taste, the way her nose crinkled a little when she bit into a tart piece of pineapple. He liked how she relaxed with the staff. He liked the quick, almost secret smiles she gave him.

Actually, he liked pretty much everything about her and the knowledge concerned him. Was he rushing into this? Getting in too deep and too fast? Probably so.

Why couldn't he be like most guys, just relax and enjoy what was going on? One reason was because he was an idiot who couldn't forget rejections—from his father's on—which meant he was living in the past. *That* made him really stupid.

"I know there's research about colors and mood," the psych resident said. "I think the right colors would help *my* mood."

"As I remember, they didn't pay enough to interest a good artist," Olivia said. "I think that was the problem."

"Hey, what's going on?" Mitchelson strode into the room. "I'm out there doing all the work myself while you guys are in here eating my birthday cake?" He looked at the one-inch square and the couple of pecans that were left. "You devoured almost the whole thing. I haven't even had a bite."

"Okay." Ana stepped in. "Let's get back to work and let Mitchelson finish his cake."

They all groaned but immediately tossed their plates in the trash and left, everyone except Ana, who grabbed Mike's arm at the doorway.

"What do you think, Mike?" she whispered.

"What do I think about what? About how pretty you are?"

"No." She slapped his hand. "About the mural painting."

What was she talking about? He shook his head.

"As a job for your mother. Do you think she'd like to paint murals at the hospital?"

"I hadn't even connected the two. Probably concentrating too much on you." He took her hand. "You're a very nice person."

"Well, I've been thinking about her. I know it would make everyone's life better if she had a job."

"You've been thinking about me, too?"

"Fuller." She ignored his question, looking confused and cute. "Why don't you check into this? I'll give her a recommendation."

"Yes, Dr. Ramírez. I'll get right on that." He glanced around. When he saw no one in the hall, he took her hand. "Do you want to go out for dinner before my shift tomorrow?"

"Love to." That terrific smile appeared. "Why don't I pack some sandwiches? We can go to Zilker Park." She turned away and said, "See you later," over her shoulder.

While he watched her walk down the hall, a hand landed on his shoulder. Oh, yeah. Mitchelson. Too bad Mike hadn't remembered the big man was finishing off the cake, but when he was with Ana, he wasn't aware of anything or anyone else.

"Is the picnic in the park completely professional, too? Like the cup of coffee?" Mitchelson dropped his hand as Mike turned toward him.

"Not exactly," Mike said. "But keep it quiet, would you? I don't want this to end up as hospital gossip."

"I promise I will, but, from the way the two of you look at each other, even if I don't say anything, the grapevine will pick it up in a day or two." Mitchelson ran his hand along the cake plate for the last bit of glaze. "That smiling thing between you two gives everything away."

Yeah, that smiling thing did give them away, but Mike was so happy he couldn't help it.

When Mike picked Ana up in the lobby of her building, he gave her a quick hug. He looked great in khaki slacks and a blue shirt. She leaned into him, feeling his warmth and the strength of his arms. He smelled like mint toothpaste, that musky aftershave and chicken.

No, the chicken scent was coming from the picnic basket.

"I'm pretty sure I can guess, but what are we having?" he asked as he took the food from her.

"I picked up some fried chicken and potato salad at Randalls grocery."

"We can get cold drinks at the park. We should be set."

Once settled in the car, she said, "Did you get a chance to go to the employment office today?"

He grinned as he turned toward the Mo-Pac. "Uh-huh. Imagine my surprise when I discovered someone else had been there before me."

Oops.

"You know, there are some things I can take care of myself," he said.

Busted. She thought she'd been so inconspicuous, so devious. "I didn't even ask anyone. Much. I looked at the board, but the job to paint the murals wasn't posted so I asked the clerk if it was still open. That's all."

"Yes, but when two people on the same day ask the same clerk about a job that's been open for almost a year, she's bound to notice."

"I'm sorry, Mike. I wanted to find out. I was curious."

"You did it because you care. I appreciate that, but you don't have to do everything for everyone."

She sighed. "It's a bad habit of mine."

"Yes, but it's one of the reasons I l— like you."

What had he meant to say? Certainly not, "I love

you." They'd only been together for a few weeks, hardly enough time to be sure of such an emotion.

"What did you find out?" she asked, still wondering about his words but deciding she didn't need to follow up, not now. "About the job."

"It was never filled because, like Olivia remembered, it pays only $6.50 an hour for twenty-five hours a week. It's short-term and has no benefits. That's about $160 a week minus taxes. The clerk said they'd hoped maybe it would appeal to a student."

She turned to study his profile. "What do you think about this job for your mother? Would the salary be enough?"

"I picked up an application. If they'd hire her, I think it would work." He took the Barton Springs exit and stopped at a light. "She'd get a work history and bring in some money. One hundred dollars a week would help a lot, and she'd enjoy it. Right now, that's really important to me."

"Mike." This was not going to be an easy question to ask, but she needed to know this, both for recommending his mother to the personnel office and because of her father's interest in Tessie. "I don't know how to ask this, but how in the world did your mother end up painting forgeries? She seems so nice."

"That's exactly the reason. She's a nice person and a great mom." He started forward with the traffic as the light changed. "I told you my family has a bad history. My uncles both served time." He drove a block without speaking.

"My father left us after Tim was born," he said. "Mom had no work skills. She lost every job because one of us got sick and she had to stay home or because she was so scatterbrained." He turned toward Ana. "I love her, but Mom has no common sense. I think Tim inherited that gene, too."

"Those years must have been hard, on all of you."

"Yeah."

He didn't elaborate but she hardly expected him to.

"Her original paintings didn't sell so she started forging to bring in money. After a few years, she got caught." He shrugged. "She really is a great person. I don't want her to go back to crime or jail." He pulled into a parking space near the trail next to the soccer fields. "Now, tell me about your family."

"We're really pretty ordinary." She got out of the car when he opened her door. "My father's family came to Texas about seventy years ago. Dad and Mom were both born here and are both citizens. They met in high school and got married when they graduated. Nothing exciting."

He bought them a drink to share at a concession booth and headed toward the picnic tables with the basket.

"You all speak Spanish." When they reached a table in the shade, he placed the food and the soft drink there.

"Yes, we're very lucky. We were brought up speaking both English and Spanish. That was a wonderful gift."

After eating and watching the soccer game between two teams of ten-year-old boys and girls, Mike suggested they walk to the botanical gardens.

"I don't like to walk that far," she protested.

"Your leg?"

"It's fine. That's not the reason. I'm tired. I work too hard to wander around in the wilderness. It's hot." She grimaced. "I'm not an athlete."

"No excuses, Doctor. You know the importance of exercise, and you don't have to be an athlete to walk through the gardens." When he teased her and smiled, she couldn't resist him. Well, she couldn't resist much about him except that Leave-me-alone-I-don't-want-to-talk-about-it mood, but she saw much less of it now.

"Oh, all right." When she put her hand in his, he pulled her to her feet.

Crossing Stratford Drive and walking along the

road, they strolled through the nearly empty parking lot to the entrance. After checking the map at the information kiosk, Mike asked, "Do you want to visit the dinosaur garden?"

"I loved it when I was a kid. We came here every summer because it was cheap."

"Free is always good," Mike said.

"But I'd like to see some of the other gardens. Let's start with the rose garden."

They wandered down a path surrounded by lush vegetation; the delicious scent of spice drifted to them on the breeze.

"Basil." Ana read the sign in the bed of plants.

As they strolled down steps at the entrance to the rose garden, they stood under the trellis covered with luxurious climbers of white and brilliant pink. Down a few more steps, they entered the garden and were surrounded by pink tea roses, multicolored blooms of apricot and gold, soft pink, yellow and deep lavender. Bushes showed brilliant coral and creamy white flowers. Ana reached down to rub the velvety petal of a dark orange tea rose.

"It smells wonderful." She lifted her head. "If I didn't know better, I'd think there were fruit trees in here."

"And tea." Mike put his arm around her. "Do you smell a strong tea scent?"

Another couple, the only people Ana had seen so far, sat on the other side of the garden. She and Mike ambled across a bridge and into the Oriental Garden, past ponds with golden koi flashing deep in the water and through the carefully laid out paths, small pagodas, large ferns and flowering plants.

After a few minutes of wandering, Mike pointed to the west. "There's a little path," he said. "Let's see where it goes. I don't remember. It's been so long since I've been here."

With his arm comfortably settled around her shoulders, they sauntered past beds of trailing lantana and up the path to a sign that pointed toward the Pioneer Village.

They walked by a red barn, blacksmith's shop, the school and the wishing well until, immediately ahead of them was a small gazebo. The lattice walls were pristinely white, its roof showing red through the trees.

"Let's go inside and rest," Mike suggested. "There's a bench here, too, around the inside. Years ago, Tim and I used to run around in there. Come on." He tugged her toward the gazebo. "I want to show you something inside."

"Oh?" Ana asked curiously. She didn't remember anything inside the gazebo. Of course, she hadn't been there for years, either. He pulled her along the trail and into the summerhouse.

"What did you want to show me?" she asked.

"This." He turned her to face him, keeping his arm around her shoulder, and studied her face for a few seconds. The tenderness in his eyes made her breathless.

"What?" she whispered.

"This." He leaned forward, very slowly, and placed his lips against hers, then put his other arm around her and pulled her into the embrace.

It started as a gentle coming together, his lips soft against hers. Slowly, it became a wow of a kiss when he shifted a little so they were even closer. She felt his warmth where she fit into his arms, surrounded by the fragrant air and the promise of his kiss.

She was lost in his loving touch. Around them, leaves whispered in the wind. For a while she was aware of the floral scents of roses and spice heavy in the air and the sound of birds singing. While she was wrapped in his embrace, all that disappeared until she felt only his arms holding her and his lips against hers.

When he heard the sound of other visitors on the path down the hillside, Mike pulled away, although they stood only inches apart. Smiling down at her, he took a tendril of her hair and curled it around his finger. "That was nice." Then he smiled and took her hand.

On her part, Ana wasn't sure she could say a coherent—or incoherent—word or walk next to him on legs made wobbly by that embrace. However, not a woman to give in to weakness, she took the hand he held out, stiffened her spine and forced herself up the path with Mike. After only a few steps, she felt her brain restart after she'd feared it might have ceased to function forever.

"Nice," she said, "doesn't begin to describe that."

"No, it doesn't, but that was the only word I could think of at the time." He turned to look at her. "You dazzle me, Ana."

She couldn't believe Mike Fuller was talking like that. He dazzled her, too.

After another enchanted hour during which they'd strolled through the rest of the gardens with kisses stolen by a pagoda or a bench overlooking the rose garden or in the butterfly center, he took her home. Once they reached the door to her apartment, Mike put his hand high on the wall and leaned above her. "Go to church with me Sunday?"

The question easily shook Ana out of her infatuated state. "Mike, I prefer not to talk about church. I'm happy as I am."

He took his hand from the wall and cupped it under her chin, lifting her face to look into his. "Ana, I have a gift of great worth I want to share with you. I hope you'll come with me."

"Mike, I—"

He leaned forward to kiss her tenderly. "Please, Ana."

"Okay," she murmured against his lips.

When he gave her a final hug and turned to catch the elevator, she shouted, "Fuller, you don't play fair."

He didn't, not at all, but she didn't hold that against him. How could she when he made her so happy in every other way?

Once inside her apartment, she tossed her purse on the entrance table and threw herself on the sofa. Was she falling in love with him? Yes, she was.

He was gorgeous. His good looks had drawn her first: the rare smile, the broad shoulders, the great hair. Then she'd seen him with children, a real eye-opener. Mike cared so deeply for them and the affection was returned. When she'd found out about how he gave up his dream to take in his family, she recognized what a fine person he was. Now she knew he was a really great kisser.

She wasn't falling in love. She'd already

landed there and was happier than she'd ever thought she could be.

Mike decided to stop at home to see his mother before he headed to work. He was in a great mood. He'd kissed Ana, the best kisses ever. And, oh, yes, he had a work application for his mother. Before he went into the house, he tried to look not quite so dazzled. Had he really told Ana she dazzled him? He never talked about his feelings and not in words like that.

Once he had settled his features to show a glimmer of intelligence instead of the absolute goofiness that had covered his features when he'd looked in the rearview mirror, he entered the house. Inside, his mother was seated on the sofa and sketching with pastels. He sat down next to her. "Mom, there may be a job at the hospital for you."

"For me?" She dropped her chalk. "In the hospital? A job?"

He nodded.

"Tell me."

"Painting murals."

"Painting murals? Painting?" Tears gathered in her eyes. "Oh, Mike, I'd love that."

"It doesn't pay much."

"Would it bring in enough money to help? You must think so or we wouldn't be talking about it."

"Yes, Mom, I think it might work. With taxes and withholding, you'd bring home over a hundred dollars a week. That would help a lot."

"Go on." She took his arm and held tightly.

"It's also short-term."

"That would give me some experience to list for another job." She nodded. "What do you think?"

"It would be perfect for you."

"Oh, Mike, I agree." The smile faded. "But I'm an ex-con."

"Dr. Ramírez says she doesn't think it would be a problem. You should call your parole officer to discuss it, then he can talk to the human resources office."

She put her hands over her face and began to sob, her shoulders shaking. He hugged her, handed her a tissue, then stood and started out of the room.

"I never thought I could make honest money painting. I'm so happy."

Why in the world did women cry when they were happy?

After getting off her next twenty-four-hour shift which had turned into a thirty-hour shift due to a three-car pileup on I-35, Ana got in her car and headed toward her father's house.

What did Papi want to talk to her about? She'd asked when he called this morning, but he wouldn't say more than, "Would you come home to talk to me after work?"

Why would he want to talk to her on this bright Saturday morning when she'd fixed him dinner just a few days earlier? Not that she'd really expected him to tell her. Although he was different around Tessie, he was pretty much the same as usual with his family, not communicating unless absolutely necessary. Had he gone to the doctor and gotten some bad news? Maybe something had happened to Martín or one of her other older siblings, something Papi needed to pass on.

"Hola, querida." He kissed her when she came in. With his back straight and a buoyant stride that was new to him, he led her to the family room. Once she was seated on the sofa, he settled in his recliner.

For a few minutes, they didn't talk. She glanced around the familiar room, every bit of which brought back strong memories of Mama and the family: the worn rug where Quique had played with his toy race cars; the ragged side of the sofa damaged by generations of stray cats Mama had taken in; the pictures Luz had drawn on the wall in crayon, painted over but still showing a little to anyone who knew they were there.

"What's up, Papi?" she asked when he didn't say anything. She studied his face. He looked years younger than he had only a few months earlier.

"You know how much I loved your mother, don't you? You know when she died, I thought my life was over."

"Of course I do. She was the center of our family." She felt a pang of sorrow. "We all loved her. It was hard for all of us, but much more difficult for you and the younger children."

"She was the love of my youth. I remember when I first saw her, sitting in algebra class, her hand up, always wanting to answer the questions." He smiled at the memory. "You were so alike, both so smart."

"Yes, Papi." With that beginning, Ana decided this conversation wouldn't be about anyone's health. She could relax.

"I never thought I'd love anyone again, but I do, Ana. I've fallen in love with Mrs. Fuller, with Tessie, and I wanted to tell you that."

She sat back in the seat. Oh, she'd known Papi found Tessie attractive. That he had fallen in love surprised her although she could see why he had. Tessie was a lovely, vibrant woman. Still, this was a shock. "She's so different from Mama."

"I know. Your mother was quiet and shy. You may have noticed, Tessie isn't like that." He laughed. "Even though she's had difficult times, Tessie's exciting and very special. She brought me back to life."

"I'm glad. I worried about you after Mama died."

He smiled sadly. "I worried about myself, too, but no longer."

She waited, allowing her father to bring up whatever it was he wanted to say.

After a false start, Papi said, "I had trouble at first because of Tessie's record. I'd never met anyone who'd been to prison, except your uncle."

"That's hard. I mean, in a relative, it's one thing, but to choose to care for someone with a criminal past, to accept it, must be difficult."

"It has been. I had to think it through very carefully. I was attracted to Tessie before I knew about her past, but it still threw me when she told me. I thought about what her record meant for me and you children and the grandchildren."

"What did she think of that?"

"Fortunately, she understood my hesitation and gave me time. As I thought about her, I realized she was a woman who struggled her whole life, who grew up in a family where honesty wasn't a value. In the end, she made a bad choice to earn money to care for her family."

"And now?"

"Now that I understand her better, I decided to look at the woman she is becoming instead of the person she was." He leaned forward. "I love her, Ana. I accept her completely. I hope you can, as well."

She had no choice. Her father had made that clear so she nodded. "Of course. What does the rest of the family think?"

"I haven't talked to them yet. I wanted to start with you because you were so close to your mother."

"But I'd never want you to be unhappy and lonely because Mama and I were close." She stood and walked across the room to sit on the arm of his chair. "I love you."

She hugged him and felt the tension leave his body.

"Thank you for understanding," he said.

"Are you going to get married?"

He smiled, a really happy smile. "That question, *mija,* is much too nosy."

Chapter Thirteen

No, Ana hadn't wanted to come to church; however, the service wasn't too bad after all. She sat next to Mike, which was worth the trip. Down the pew were Julie from the diner, Francie and Brandon, Tim, Tessie, in a dark blue and much more conservative but still-spangled dress, and Ana's father. Quite a group.

The music was nice, the sanctuary had lovely windows, and, well, she was with Mike.

Those qualities she'd noticed about him when they first met—the edge to his personality, a nervousness which made him a little intimidating, and, of course, that closed-off expression—had disappeared in this place. He was at peace. A changed Mike, but still as attractive.

Not that she should notice the magnetism

between them at church. At church, she should follow his example, and he was completely involved in the service. So she stood with him for the opening chorus, bowed her head during the prayer, met and chatted with others during the greeting time and smiled when the children sang.

To her surprise, the sermon was thoughtful and interesting. She'd always thought they'd be long and boring with little substance. Probably the prejudice of a person who didn't go to church. Even in the large sanctuary, she felt an intimacy, as if the minister were talking to her, which she found a completely comfortable situation.

At the end of the service, many members of the congregation stopped to talk to Mike's family and introduced themselves to her. Everyone was friendly and invited her to return.

All in all, the morning was not horrible. If Mike asked her, she'd come back with him. If she came back to church just to be with Mike, did that make her attendance a sin? Perhaps God would like her to come back to church whatever the reason.

After Tessie had been painting for two weeks, the murals were the talk of the hospital. Patients and staff gathered to watch Tessie paint and to praise what she'd finished. She'd completed one with dogs and cats playing on a vibrant green background in pediatrics.

In the E.R. waiting room, using soothing colors, she was painting a mural of a garden. The receptionist said it not only calmed the patients and their families but made *her* feel a lot more peaceful.

Not that Tessie had limited her hours to twenty-five a week. "I can't," she'd explained to Mike when he reminded her how much time she was spending at the hospital. "Once I start painting, I don't want to stop and clean up. Once the creativity is flowing, I need to follow it." She stroked her hands through the air, her brush dripping ochre paint on the drop cloth. "I never know where the muse will lead."

In a structure built to alleviate pain, the paintings brought a healing influence. Joy lifted some of the sorrow and hope replaced a few moments of fear. Mike believed his mother was inspired, that God worked through her to heal, but he didn't mention it to her. Mom's faith wasn't ready for that yet.

One evening before his shift began, Mike entered the waiting room to see his mother putting the final touches to the garden mural, painting a deep shadow on the edge of a rose petal, a dab of white against the sky. As usual, she wore old jeans with one of his old shirts. And, as usual, Mr. Ramírez sat in a chair watching her every move.

"Isn't she talented?" He turned toward Mike, beaming proudly.

"I've always known she was."

His mother didn't notice either him or Mr. Ramírez, too wrapped up in her creations.

A week later, Ana searched in her purse for the key to her apartment. When she found it, Mike put it in the lock and opened the door.

"Thanks for a great lunch," she said.

He wished he could say something romantic and flowery. But every word seemed to stick in his throat and jam up in his mouth if he tried.

"Yeah. Great," he said instead.

She smiled. "I wish you didn't have to work the early shift, but I'll see you later."

He gave her a quick kiss.

Without bothering to take the elevator, he just ran down the stairs filled with happiness and energy. Life was terrific. Tim had gone to the recruiting office last week, taken a test and was pretty much set to leave for basic training in four months. Before that, he had to meet with the recruiting officer to set things up, but it sounded as if Tim's life and plans were set for a few years.

His mother's creations filled several walls of the hospital. On top of her success, she'd received a raise and an increase in hours to thirty a week. She and Mr. Ramírez were happily courting. When Mike'd asked her if they were getting serious, she'd laughed and waved her hands but given no information. A true Fuller.

The best part, what made him happiest, was Ana. She'd gone with him to church for two more weeks. He knew she'd gone with him the first time to please him, but *she* had reminded him last week to pick her up Sunday. More surprisingly, they'd discussed faith a few times. She was still skeptical but had been willing to listen and ask questions.

All in all, life was good. His family seemed on the right track and he was in love.

Yeah, no use denying it. He was in love and very pleased about it. She was the right woman for him: smart, pretty and caring. Their interest in medicine gave them a strong tie. When he looked back, he realized how shallow the relationship between him and Cynthia had been, based on her beauty and his future. He'd liked to show Cynthia off, amazed that a woman like her could love little Mike Fuller, son of an ex-con. She liked to say, "Mike's in medical school."

Ana accepted him as who he was—well, except that one thing. He didn't communicate well. He'd never been able to, but, as long as life was good, he didn't have to dwell on those old hurts or hide those parts of him he didn't want to share with anyone. He could bury them deep where they wouldn't bother anyone.

He believed Ana cared for him. They were together as often as they could work out. They had fun, as well as interesting conversations. And he really, really liked to kiss her.

By the time he saw Ana at work that evening, he wasn't feeling nearly as great as he had earlier. His head was pounding and his joints felt as if he'd been stomped on by a herd of orderlies. Did he have a temperature? He thought so but didn't want to know. If he did have one, he'd probably feel worse.

Ana didn't let him off as easily. She watched him during staff change, then charged toward him when she saw him in the hall.

"Stand still." She put her hand against his forehead. "Olivia, get Fuller's temperature."

He was running a fever of 101.

Ana put her hands on her hips and glared at him. "Why are you here? Don't you realize your illness jeopardizes both patients and staff?"

"But I can't go home. I need—"

"Listen, Fuller, I'm speaking as Dr. Ramírez so you have to listen to me. Go home now."

Not strong enough to argue and knowing he'd lose anyway, he nodded, went into the staff locker room and got his billfold and keys.

"Okay, what's the matter with you?" Ana entered the room behind him. Now she was both the professional Dr. Ramírez and his girlfriend, a difficult balancing act.

"Headache." He put his hand on his forehead. "Weak and achy."

"Go home. Drink plenty of water and sleep. Take some aspirin to bring down the temperature if your stomach can handle it." She shook her finger in front of him. "Don't come back until you're not contagious and," she said in a softer voice, "until you feel a lot better."

She glanced around the room, stood on her tiptoes and kissed him on the cheek. "Go on. Get in bed and get well."

"I'll be back tomorrow," he said in an effort at humor that didn't work at all. He gave her a pathetic grin and headed for the parking lot.

It was almost midnight when he got home. As he drove down the street, he saw a movement in the bushes next to the window of the bedroom he and Tim shared.

Was someone trying to get in? Not that they had anything worth stealing, but Mom and Tim were in there. He wished he had a cell phone, but his was in the house for everyone to use.

He turned off the headlights and pulled up a few houses past theirs. Making as little noise as possible, he opened the door and slid out. Ignoring his shaky legs, he hunkered down and crept silently around the neighbor's yard and through his backyard.

When he could see between the houses, the shadow moved and became a person. He sneaked closer to the figure of a man who looked a few inches shorter than he and about thirty pounds lighter. He could probably take him if he had to. Well, maybe if the intruder was also suffering from the flu and had the strength of lettuce, Mike could take him.

Mike slid behind a crepe myrtle to see if the man was breaking in, but he had to lean against the wall to rest for a few seconds first.

No, the prowler had placed the screen against the house—had he already been inside?—and was moving away from it. He had nothing in his hands, but he could have hurt the family. Should Mike check inside the house or chase the man? He'd never catch him, not with his legs still shaking. He couldn't climb in the window due to his painful joints, so he watched.

As the figure reached the front yard, a car drove

up, a dark SUV with silver flames on the side. When the man ran toward it, Mike recognized the jacket in the illumination of the streetlight. It was his. Then he recognized Tim's familiar lope and ran after him as fast as he could, which matched the speed of an arthritic snail.

"What in the world do you think you're doing?" Mike said as Tim opened the door of the SUV. "Tim, get back here."

Tim froze. Mike hadn't ever seen anyone freeze like this except in a movie. It was as if the words had fallen over his head and down his body like a blanket of ice.

"Tim, come here."

Tim turned toward his brother but didn't move closer.

"Hey, are you coming?" a male voice asked from the SUV.

"Go on." Tim closed the door and waved toward the driver. "Get out of here."

The tires squealed as the car took off. Step by hesitant step, Tim moved closer to the house. Mike expected him to say, "I can explain," but he didn't.

"Do you want to tell me what's going on?" Mike asked.

He was beginning to feel even worse. With the adrenaline rush when he believed his family was in danger, he'd been able to function. Now the headache throbbed so much he felt as if someone were driving a spike through his eye. He was so weak he had to hold on to the porch column to stay on his feet. Slowly he sank to the ground.

"Hey, what's the matter?" Tim leaned over his brother.

"Don't change the subject." Mike stared up at him from his position on the grass and made an effort to sound intimidating. "Where were you going?"

Tim put his hand on Mike's forehead. "You're hot. You're really sick."

"Where were you going?" He wished he could go to bed instead of carrying on this conversation. Sweat dripped down his forehead and body. When a light, warm breeze hit him, it nearly knocked him over. He shivered.

"You should be in bed."

"Tell me the truth. I'd rather be in bed, but I'm not going to do that until I find out more." Although he feared he might die first.

"A bunch of us were going for a drive."

"A ride after midnight? Don't kid me. Why did you climb out of the window?"

Tim didn't answer immediately. He shifted from foot to foot, an action Mike could see very well from his seat on the ground.

"I didn't want Mom to hear me close the front door. It has a really bad squeak."

Mike's body slowly listed to the left until he allowed himself to lie prone, hardly the most threatening position. "Why?" he murmured.

"You need to go to bed."

"Tim, why?" he forced the words out.

"Rudy wanted to do some stuff."

"Rudy? The kid with the juvie record who lives two blocks over?"

"Yeah, but he's really a nice guy."

"Guns?" He couldn't talk enough to form a complete sentence.

"No, no guns." Tim sat on the ground next to his brother. "Just some fun."

"Knocking over mailboxes? That kind?"

He thought Tim nodded but, of course, with his eyes closed, he couldn't see the action. "When I'm feeling better, you're in a whole lot of trouble." After a few minutes of silence during which Mike almost fell asleep on the ground, he said, "For now, help me up." He reached out his hand for Tim to grab and pull him to his feet. They limped into the living room where Mike collapsed on the sofa, unable to go another step.

As he fell asleep, Mike had an unnerving thought. His brother had felt the call of the wild again, the terrible gene of danger that wandered through his family and had destroyed several of them. What was Mike going to do to stop that?

Obviously nothing tonight.

Three days passed before Mike was able to get to his feet for longer than a few minutes. Ana had visited the day after he'd left the hospital sick. First she greeted his mother, who was hovering over Mike and driving him crazy.

As a doctor, Ana checked on him, diagnosed the disease as a virus, and told him to keep forcing liquids and stay in bed. Then, as Ana, she gave him a bunch of flowers and kissed his forehead. Nice. On the second day, she read the newspaper to him while his mother cooked his favorite food to try to tempt his appetite. It didn't work, but he appreciated the effort more than he had her pillow fluffing.

All those days he was sick, Mike had stayed on the sofa. Although it was too short for him, he didn't notice that first twenty-four hours. Then, even sick as he was, he couldn't rest in the bedroom with a two-foot-high accumulation of Tim's clothing—dirty and clean—empty soft-drink cans and other unidentifiable debris covering the floor. He didn't have the strength to pick them up. Besides, out here he could sleep through a few more baseball games.

As Mike began to feel better on the third day, Tim got sick and spent the next few days on the bottom bunk.

By the time Mike was better, he'd missed five days of work. Although he'd accumulated sick days, he couldn't use them until he'd completed the six-month probation period. That was money he couldn't make up quickly because he was in no condition to do overtime.

Tim had missed three days at the burger place so far, and their mother had missed hours of work taking care of them.

The financial situation looked bleak and was even worse when he found a check for sixty dollars their mother had written for paint supplies. He knew there was a huge charge for the antibiotic for Tim when his virus went into bronchitis. Thank goodness Ana had taken care of Tim. They could never have afforded to pay a doctor.

The evening of his fifth night off, Ana dropped by with chocolate ice cream for Mike to put some weight back on him. When she saw him, she asked, "What are you doing up and dressed?" She glared at him. "You don't plan to go to work, do you?" When he didn't answer, she glared even more fiercely. "You can't go back to work. You're too weak. You won't make it until midnight."

"I'm fine."

"Sure you are." She put a hand on his chest and pushed gently. He dropped down on the sofa. "See." She sat next to him. "Mike, this is a very serious virus. It really saps your strength. We've admitted a lot of people to the hospital."

"See, that's another reason I have to go to work." He stood. "You're not my supervisor and you're not my doctor. You can't tell me what to do."

"Oh?" Her expression hardened. "If I'm not your supervisor or doctor, what am I to you?"

It took a few seconds for both of them to realize what she'd said, really said. She'd asked about their relationship. She hadn't meant to, but it had popped out when he listed what she wasn't.

She guessed he hadn't thought the conversation would turn to this and maybe it was mean to ask him when he was so weak, but she wanted to know.

After a long pause during which he sat on the arm of the sofa and she shoved the ice cream into his hand, he said, "You're my good friend."

That's great. He considered her his good friend? "Do you often kiss your good friends?"

"Shh!" He waved his hands toward the kitchen. "Mom can hear you."

"I don't care." When she took a step toward him, he attempted to move back on the arm of the sofa until he couldn't move farther away.

"No." He cleared his throat. "You're more than that, but I don't know how to describe it. I'm not good at that, and I still feel bad."

His complexion had taken on a greenish tinge on top of the earlier pale gray. He wasn't well. He'd lost so much weight his jeans hung on him. She sighed. Even though he was playing on her sympathy, this wasn't the time to press him. Besides, she feared he'd tell her she was a nice lady next, and her ego couldn't handle that. She took pity on him and changed the subject although he wouldn't like this one, either.

"Mike, you cannot go to work tonight. As you said, I'm not your doctor, but I am *a* doctor. What I say about your condition will have influence in the E.R. A doctor has to clear you for work after this long an absence. None of them will, not after I talk to them."

An expression of relief skimmed across his face. He leaned back and closed his eyes. "Okay. One more day."

"I'll come by and check on you tomorrow. If you're stronger, I'll clear you, but no overtime until I say so."

"Yes, Doctor." He opened his eyes and grinned.

"I'm going to check on Tim while I'm here." She headed toward the bedroom.

"You're a really nice person," Mike mumbled before he fell asleep, still sitting on the sofa with his head resting against the wall.

Not as bad as being a nice lady, but she still wished she hadn't heard those words.

Chapter Fourteen

The next day, Mike felt stronger, but Ana couldn't drop by and check on him. She'd called that morning to tell him she'd now caught the virus, as well, had left the E.R. early and was at her father's home where the family could take care of her.

He consoled her until she stopped speaking and he heard a sharp voice on the other end of the line.

"Ana, you go to bed, now." After a pause, the same voice said, "Hi, Mike, this is Luz. My stubborn sister almost fell asleep while you were talking so I sent her to bed."

"How's she doing? Really."

"Probably about the same as you were on your first day of this stuff." She sighed. "She's the worst patient you can imagine."

"Really?" he asked, not a bit surprised.

"She's so hardheaded. She *knows* she can do anything if she pushes hard enough. She hates being weak, so this is really tough on her, but it's worse on the family."

"I'm sorry for all of you."

There was a pause while Mike heard Luz put a hand over the phone and say, "Get back in bed or I'll drag you there." Then she said to Mike, "Bye," and hung up.

After he showered, shaved and got dressed, he looked in on Tim. The kid had really been sick but that wasn't going to save him from a reaming out as soon as Tim could stay awake for five minutes and as soon as he could force himself to do that.

Mom fixed him breakfast, a nice bowl of oatmeal with brown sugar. For the first time in days, Mike had an appetite.

"May I have another?" He spooned the cereal into his mouth, finished that and held the bowl out. "Please."

"Of course. I've got to get some weight back on you." She placed the second serving in front of him. "I want you to rest until it's time to go to work."

He wanted to protest, but it would be childish. She was right. Maybe that was what becoming an adult was: recognizing that what your mother said made sense. Occasionally.

Breakfast finished and the dishes washed, he went back into the bedroom he and Tim shared and began to pick up clothes, dishes and stuff he preferred not to identify. Once he could walk across the floor without tripping, he pulled the sheets off Tim, who groaned but didn't wake up, and dumped them in the laundry bag with the clothes to take to the Soap and Spin.

"Mom," he shouted from the front door, "You'll need to put clean sheets on Tim's bed. I'm taking these to the Laundromat." He escaped before she could say anything.

By noon, he had a pile of clean laundry but had begun to wish he'd listened to his mother. When he got home, he carried the basket inside. Before he could do more, he dropped on the sofa and fell asleep.

Waking up when his mother called felt like struggling up through deep mud. He lay on the sofa for a few minutes, forcing himself to move, but his body refused to respond.

"It's seven-thirty, Mike." She stood at the arch into the kitchen. "I have your dinner ready and your lunch packed. Are you going to see Ana before you go to the hospital?"

He nodded.

"Good. Antonio wants me to come over. I'll go

with you and he'll drive me home." She smiled and her eyes shone with joy.

Everyone was conspiring against her, enjoying her weakened state. Luz had left at noon and put her in the unsympathetic hands of Martita. Her sister-in-law had given her a sponge bath when Ana wanted a shower. This request had been refused *only* because Ana couldn't stand on legs made treacherously unsteady by this stupid illness.

Then Martita, the devious woman, had given her a back rub that lulled Ana to sleep. She napped until almost four o'clock. Now, since Mike had called to say he'd be by on the way to the hospital, she wanted to get up and get dressed, but Martita and her father had refused to allow it.

Martita washed Ana's face again, helped her put on makeup over Ana's loud protests that she could do it herself. That completed, Martita had swaddled her in a warm gown and robe, helped her into a chair in the living room and tossed a blanket over her. As if she couldn't walk to the living room herself. Of course she could, although there had been that one little trip over the edge of the throw rug. She'd never noticed how dangerous that spot was before.

Then Mike had arrived. With a kiss on the cheek, he'd awakened her from yet another nap.

"You're so skinny." Oh, bother. She could feel tears gather in her eyes. What an idiot she was, so sentimental, so emotional. She hated being sick. "I'm glad to see you."

He handed her a tissue.

"I don't need that." She waved it away. "I'm not crying. I never cry."

Why did everyone smile when she said that?

"Querida," her father said. Why would he call her his darling when she was acting like such a cranky person? "You're sick. You can cry over nothing when you're sick."

"While you were asleep," Martita said, "Francie brought you some of Manny's chicken soup. I'll fix you a cup later."

"How nice." She lay back and put her arm over her eyes so no one could see the tears.

"Honey, it's okay." Mike kneeled on the rug in front of the sofa, gently moved her arm aside and blotted her cheeks with the tissue. "You're human."

"What a terrible thing to say."

"You can't reason with her," Martita said. "I've always heard doctors were the worst patients. Don't we know that."

After a few minutes, Mike stood and his mother

took his place, brushing Ana's hair back and cooing soothingly.

"Ana, I've got to get going to the hospital. I'll be back tomorrow. What can I bring you?"

"Just you," she said. "Don't overwork yourself. Rest whenever you can."

"Yes, Dr. Ramírez." He laughed and headed outside.

Ana closed her eyes. She had a virus. It would take a few days to shake it, but soon she'd be as healthy as Mike.

But, oh, how she hated to be sick.

The next few days were a nightmare for Mike. It had been a killer virus, as Ana had said. Still not at full strength, he struggled through an eight-hour shift, then went home, called Ana. After that, he'd go to bed and sleep until noon. His mom awakened him for lunch, he read his anatomy book until he dozed off and slept until she woke him up again at eight to eat and go see Ana.

He was so tired when he went into work at ten-thirty he wondered how he'd make it. He had no illusions he could work a double shift. With Tim sick, his younger brother wasn't earning a penny. Fortunately, he was well enough for Mom to work her full thirty hours, but they were so far behind financially.

He hadn't discussed the paint and supplies Tessie had bought. They'd work that out.

What he dreaded most was that he still hadn't talked to Tim about his sneaking out of the house the night Mike got sick. He didn't want to. Confrontation was his least favorite thing in the world. Mike preferred withdrawal, and he knew Tim well enough to know his little brother would make the conversation as difficult as possible.

When Mike got home after his second night back at work, he pulled out the checkbook and looked at his budget. They were okay now, but after he paid the bills there wouldn't be enough money and not much coming in. He'd have to take money from his savings, which would wipe out that account. He dropped his head in his hands. He'd have to work overtime or they wouldn't be able to eat.

He could take the bus home from work, but not to work because there were no connections that late at night. What good would it do to have someone take him and drive home so he could save gas money taking the bus home? None of the other graveyard shift staff lived in this direction, so carpooling was out.

What was left to cut? Nothing. He'd have to work more hours.

The sound of someone moving around awakened him at ten-thirty. "Tim?"

"Yeah. I'm fixing breakfast."

He stood and went into the kitchen. "We need to talk."

"What part—" Tim bit the words off "—of 'I'm eighteen' don't you understand?"

"The part about 'I can do whatever I want and won't get into trouble with the law.' That's the part."

"I wasn't going to get in trouble." He slid the eggs from the skillet onto his plate. "We were going to drive around, that's all."

"No throwing eggs? No paint cans? No vandalism?"

Tim shook his head and shoved two pieces of bread in the toaster.

"Did anyone have a gun?"

"How would I know? You didn't even let me get into the car."

"Tim, you could have ignored me. You could have gotten into that car, but you didn't. That makes me feel that deep down you knew whatever was going to happen wasn't what you wanted, really wanted, to do."

Instead of leaving the kitchen, Tim sat down and began to spread peanut butter on his toast.

"Was there beer involved?" Mike asked.

Tim frowned. "You know I'm not old enough."

"Like that's ever stopped a kid."

Tim shrugged and took a bite of toast.

"Playing chicken?" Mike asked.

"Driving fast, most likely. Maybe shooting paintballs. I don't know." He chewed and swallowed. "I didn't go."

"How many times have you sneaked out?"

"A couple." He slapped the table with his fist. "You don't know how hard it is to make friends when you're out of school. Everyone I work with is going to college. The Montoyas live on the other side of town, and we have only one car."

"I know that's tough."

"Sure you do." He stood. "You're Super-Mike. You're smart. You're good-looking. You make friends easily. How would you know?" He turned, took a step and tossed the dishes toward the sink. "Everyone says I should be like you, hardworking, responsible, never get in trouble." He scowled. "Well, I'll never be as smart or good as you so I might as well give up trying."

"What are you talking about?"

"You know, Mr. Perfect."

Mike got up and followed Tim into the bedroom they shared. "I'm not Mr. Perfect."

"Sure."

"Tim, I did something really stupid, something criminal when I was eighteen." He leaned against the wall. "I got someone I really love in trouble for that, and I'll never forgive myself."

"What?" Tim swiveled to look at him. "What did you do?"

"I can't tell you."

Tim took off and tossed his T-shirt in the direction of the hamper. "Then I bet it didn't happen. You're making that up to scare me."

"No, I'm not. Believe me. I can't tell you because the person I hurt, the person who ended up taking the blame made me swear never to tell anyone." He put his hands in his pocket. "I broke that promise once for a good reason, and that person got very angry with me. I'm not going to do it again."

Tim ambled over and leaned against the wall facing Mike. "You really messed up? You know what it's like?"

"I was as short as you were in high school, didn't grow until I was a senior. I lived with six or seven foster families in different parts of towns and gave up trying to make friends or playing varsity basketball—and I was a great shooting guard. Yeah, Tim, I know what it's like. Being a teenager is hard."

"Oh." Tim nodded. "Okay, I'll think about what you said." He slipped into his flip-flops and headed toward the bathroom before he turned around and said, "But I'm eighteen and I can leave this house whenever I want to. You can't stop me."

That hadn't gone as well as he'd hoped, but it was going to have to be enough.

When Mike got home, he fell on the sofa and slept so deeply he didn't hear Tim go to work or Mr. Ramírez drop his mother off from the hospital. He did hear her come in and close the door quietly.

"Mom, I need to talk to you." Still half-asleep, he sat up and glanced at his watch. Whoa, almost five o'clock in the afternoon. He'd napped for nine hours.

She twirled to the couch, smiling and happy, and reached down to touch his cheek. "How are you feeling? Your cheek feels cool." Then she sat beside him. "But you look tired."

"I made it." But was he ever thankful he didn't have a double shift today. "Mom, I need to talk to you about the money you spent for paint."

"I should have talked to you when I bought it. I'm sorry."

"Just tell me about it. Wasn't the hospital supposed to buy your supplies?"

"Yes, but you know the hospital purchasing procedure. I knew I was going to run out of paint two weeks ago, just before you got sick. I filled out a purchase order request but it would take a week to process and another a week to ship." She shrugged. "I had no paint or brushes and wouldn't for weeks. I decided it was better to spend the money so I could work and make money than to take time off." She patted his hand. "I'm sorry. You got sick and I forgot."

"It's okay, Mom. We'll cover it somehow."

That meant he'd have to do a double shift tomorrow. He'd be stronger by then. He had to be.

Chapter Fifteen

For Mike, the best thing about the double shift was seeing Ana during his evening break. When he drove over to her house to take her a milk shake, he was glad she felt better but worried because she was determined to work part of her next shift. Of course, there was no reasoning with her.

The worst part about the double shift? Simply that it *was* a double shift. By ten in the evening, he had to take a vertical nap. During a lull at 4:00 a.m., he crashed for thirty minutes in the lounge. An hour before he could go home, a sheen of perspiration covered his face and his legs had taken on an unsteady life of their own. The attending physician took one look at him and told him to go home immediately. Mike didn't argue.

After a quick call to Ana, he hit the lower bunk

and slept until three-thirty that afternoon. Groaning when the alarm went off, he wished he hadn't promised to take the second half of an afternoon shift.

Nine hours of sleep. He felt stronger, but he wished he could sleep nine more hours. That would give him the final shove he needed to be completely well. What he had now was an ephemeral kind of strength sure to desert him by midnight. He'd have to hide from Ana or she'd send him home early.

The thought of seeing Ana at the hospital stopped him right there on the edge of the bed. He dropped his head in his hands to think.

What about Ana? He loved her so much. Who wouldn't? But the relationship was way out of balance. She was smart, successful, beautiful and gave him so much. The only things he'd given her were a few kisses and the flu.

He hated the fact that his thoughts kept ending up in the same place, but with his family problems, their growing debt and his still feeling so tired physically, he struggled to find anything about himself he could offer Ana. Of course, he had his faith, which was such a huge part of his life now. But faith was one thing he and Ana *didn't* share.

"Dear Lord, thank You for all You have done.

Please give me wisdom," he whispered. When he searched his muddled thoughts to add more, he reminded himself God knew his needs. "Amen."

In spite of the prayer, his brain circled back. Would it be better to stop seeing each other until he could figure out how to handle the mounting money problems, how to juggle his mother and brother's lives plus the terrible realization he'd have to put med school off for even longer? Right now, as much as he cared about her, he couldn't face Ana's cheerful pushiness, her insistence that he *communicate.* He didn't do it well, not at all well. Couldn't she just accept that?

No, she couldn't, and he didn't want to discuss the mess that was his life with anyone.

At the hospital it was so easy to fall into the routine of kidding and chatting when they passed in the hall or had a free minute. He'd always looked for her during that time, to see if she were free, if they could spend a few minutes together. Life would be easier if he switched to another unit, if he didn't have to be close to her so often.

All in all, Mike wasn't in the best state of mind to go to the hospital. He made it through the half shift from seven to eleven fine, but it got tougher when he saw Ana during the shift change. Although pale and thinner, she looked terrific. She always looked terrific to him. That was the problem.

It would be better for them to be apart now, for him to transfer to another unit until he got his head straight and his life in order.

Ana didn't feel all that great. When she'd checked in the mirror before she left home, she'd looked as bad as she felt: dark circles under the eyes and a greenish complexion the same color Mike's had been. She wore her skinny jeans, the ones she seldom could zip but tonight they closed easily.

Once in the E.R., she revived a little but didn't feel her usual confidence or enthusiasm.

"How're you doing, Fuller?" She passed him in the hall on the way to an exam room.

He nodded. "Fine, Dr. Ramírez. Thank you."

The evening went pretty much like that. He assisted her with patients although he disappeared during a letup in the patient load. Probably helping in another section of the E.R. She was in no shape to look for him.

The hours went by slowly until finally it was close to 7:00 a.m. She'd worked one-third of her usual shift, and exhaustion had dropped over her like a lead cape. Fortunately, she had almost thirty-six hours until her next shift. During that time, she could rest and maybe see Mike this evening or for lunch the next day. The thought made her feel a lot better.

At the end of the shift change, Mike asked, "How'd it go?" when they headed out the door together.

As if he didn't know. As if he hadn't just gone through the first day back after the killer virus.

"Okay for the first shift back at work." She leaned against the wall. "I'd love to talk to you, but I've got to get home."

"Going back to bed?"

"Exactly what I'm going to do. I'm going to sleep all day." She pushed off the wall. "You had the same thing. When do you start feeling better?"

"I'm doing fine tonight. Give yourself a couple more days. Rest, drink plenty of liquids and don't push yourself."

She grinned weakly. "You sound like a doctor."

"And you're going to do exactly as I say."

"Why don't you come over tonight? To make sure I do?" she asked as he walked her to the parking lot.

He stopped walking for a second and glanced quickly down at her. "Um, can't. Sorry, I've got some stuff to do."

"Oh, okay." She could use the rest. She got in

the car, started it and headed toward the exit. Through the rearview mirror, she saw Mike watch her drive off. Then he turned back toward the hospital. He must have left something behind.

On her next shift, Ana felt much stronger, but she was *not* happy. Furious would describe her emotion better. Because she didn't see him earlier in the evening, she'd thought Mike was off duty. At 3:00 a.m., Williams said, "I'm going to pedes during my break later."

"Oh, why's that?" she asked.

"To see Fuller."

"What's Fuller doing in pedes?" Ana asked, distracted while adding notes to a patient's history. "Filling in for someone?"

"He got transferred there."

The chart clattered against the tiles when Ana dropped it. "Sorry," she said when everyone turned to look at the source of the noise. She picked up the chart but didn't ask another question. No reason to give the E.R. the juicy gossip that Dr. Ramírez hadn't known Mike transferred and was not happy—actually, she was furious—that he hadn't told her.

"How nice." She smiled. "He loves those kids."

She finished charting, placed the clipboard back

in the rack at the nurses' station and headed outside. Once there, she dialed pediatrics and asked for Fuller.

"Yes," he said when he got to the phone.

"Fuller, this is Dr. Ramírez."

Mike didn't answer for a few seconds. "Oh, hi," he said in a cheerful but uncomfortable voice.

She didn't swallow that response for a second. He wasn't a bit glad she'd called.

"I'd like to talk to you." She paused then added, "Soon," because she knew he wouldn't want to talk to her anytime, not in the near future, not in the distant future.

"Meet me in the cafeteria? Seven-thirty?" he suggested.

His complete lack of enthusiasm filled her with dread. What was going on?

Besides, the cafeteria wouldn't work. What she wanted to talk to him about might end up with a lot of yelling on her part because she could imagine the silence and control on his. "I'd prefer someplace less crowded and more private."

When he didn't make another suggestion, she said, "How 'bout the picnic area in the south lawn by the clinic?"

"All right."

"Will you be there?"

"Yes, I'll be there." But he didn't sound at all pleased about it.

Too bad.

Ana chose a bench under a post oak. To distract herself, she studied the contortions the branches of the trees made. She'd begun to look for another diversion when she saw Mike amble across the grass toward her with the eagerness of a child going to the dentist.

The man looked great. He'd put weight on so his jeans didn't hang from his hips. Strong arms swung from those broad shoulders. The breeze ruffled his hair, but he didn't smile. Not a good sign. Not at all. The sight of his grim features made her catch her breath. She felt as if someone had filled her stomach with balloons that weighed a ton each and burst every few seconds.

When he reached her, he settled at the other end of the bench leaving a good ten inches between them. He didn't show any interest in beginning the conversation. He just sat there, resting his elbows on his knees and looking toward the hospital, all of which made it very clear it was up to her to say something.

She'd never felt so confused and deflated in her life. "When did you decide to transfer to pedes?" she asked.

"Wednesday."

"Why didn't you tell me?"

He didn't look at her, not a glance. "You know I wanted to work there. I thought you'd be happy for me."

Oh, sure. Make this *her* problem. "I didn't realize…" She stopped words that had taken on a sharp edge. Confrontation wasn't the tactic she wanted to use, not with this unapproachable man. "If you thought I'd be happy, why didn't you tell me?"

He shrugged. "Didn't have time."

After a long pause, she realized she'd have to push harder. How frustrating. It was as if they'd moved months backward in their relationship. "I missed your call yesterday morning."

He shrugged again. In fact, he was shrugging so often it looked like a shoulder exercise from the Physical Therapy Department.

"Busy," he said.

This was going great. "Mike, what's going on?"

This time he turned toward her for a second. "Nothing."

She blinked. "What do you mean, nothing?"

He looked down at his hands. "Things are busy for me now."

"Do you want to talk about it?" She bit her lips

to keep from screaming at him although he deserved it. If she did, he'd just get up and walk off and she'd learn nothing. As if she was learning so much now.

"Mike, do you care for me at all?"

When he nodded, her temper flared. Bothersome, irritating man! She closed her eyes. *Dear Lord, please give me the wisdom to deal with this impossible man.*

Her eyes popped open. She'd just prayed. On her own because she wanted to. She wished she could share this experience with Mike, but he didn't want to hear anything from her. He made that clear by scooting a few more inches away from her so his body balanced on the end of the bench.

"Mike, what's going on? Do you want a relationship with me?"

He glanced at her. "Yes, but I have to take care of some things first." With that, he stood and headed toward the parking lot.

He had to take care of some things first? What was that about?

She watched him walk away and realized that, for the tiny bit of sharing, communicating and shouting they'd done, they could have had this conversation in the middle of a shift change. No one would have noticed. She had learned only that Mike was busy and was not going to tell her the tiniest bit more.

Didn't the man realize that there was *never* a time when everything was okay? That there were always rocky places in life? Even in her terrific family, there'd been tough times when someone got sick or they were short on money. Mike was asking her for an on-and-off relationship when *he* felt good, when everything was going well, an arrangement that didn't interest her at all.

She was angry. At the same time, the hurt burned so deeply inside she had to push herself to her feet.

Sunday morning, Ana tried to sleep late but awakened at seven. She read the newspaper while she ate a grapefruit and drank her coffee. That completed, it was only eight o'clock. What would she do with the rest of the morning?

Go to church.

The thought amazed her. She'd only gone three times, but church attendance had become a habit after such a short while. Was she going to allow Mike to keep her from her church? No. Never. She marched into the bedroom and began to get ready.

Arriving a few minutes early, Ana scanned the sanctuary. Mike sat next to Tim. Tessie and her father were in the middle of the pew next to Julie and Francie while Brandon sat on the end with enough space left for another person. She walked down the aisle and slid into the empty space. Brandon scooted over to make more room and smiled at her while Francie reached out to pat her hand and whisper, "Good to see you." Looking down the row, everyone else waved to her or smiled, except for Mike. She didn't think he saw her because he was so wrapped up in prayer.

He looked miserable, the idiot! It served him right. This must be as hard for him as it was for her, but it didn't need to be.

Maybe she shouldn't be here. Should she leave him in peace? No, she had a right to worship and wasn't about to leave. She relaxed, listened to the prelude and meditated.

After a lovely choir anthem, the associate minister stood, opened the Bible and said, "Reading from the Gospel according to Matthew, chapter eleven, verses twenty-eight to thirty." He cleared his throat before he read, "'Come to me, all you that are weary and are carrying heavy burdens, and I will give you rest. Take my yoke upon you, and learn from me; for I am gentle and humble in heart, and you will find rest for your souls. For my yoke is easy, and my burden is light.'"

Amazing words, healing words. Ana opened

the bulletin to the scripture and read it to herself. They made her feel peaceful and renewed. The Lord understood her pain and even took it upon Himself. What a wonderful promise. Then she closed the bulletin to listen to the sermon.

After the last hymn, Francie pulled Ana closer to her. "He's being such an idiot," Francie whispered. "Give him time."

Ana glanced down the aisle. Mike had already left, not even looking at her or talking to anyone in the pew. Right now, he was acting like such a jerk she wasn't sure she even wanted to be with him. "Francie, how are you doing? When are you due?"

"Okay, change the subject, but I'm not finished. Can't you have a little patience with him?"

"Patience isn't one of my virtues. Besides, what's going on isn't my choice."

"He's not an easy person to know, but it's worth it." She grinned. "Now, to answer your question, I'm due in two weeks and am doing great."

"'Come to me, all you that are weary and are carrying heavy burdens, and I will give you rest,'" Mike repeated to himself as he hurried from the sanctuary. Outside, he found a bench in the garden to the side of the church and sat to consider the scripture.

Since he'd found Christ, Mike had tried to be strong in order to follow the Lord, to do His work, but this morning, the words from Matthew struck him in the heart. "'Come to me, all you that are weary and are carrying heavy burdens, and I will give you rest,'" he whispered.

In the turmoil of his life, Mike had forgotten that basic promise of faith. He wasn't alone in his pain. Why was that part of Jesus's teaching so hard for him to remember? Why did he forget that if he turned his life over to his Savior, they shared the pain and burden?

The big problem came with the word *if*. Could he turn this whole mess over to Jesus? Yes, he could, but for him it would be hard to let go of every ugly corner and painful deed. He'd become pretty good at trying to hide them. Because Mike knew himself pretty well, he also knew the task wasn't going to be easy for someone who trusted as little as he did, but he could trust his Savior. That he did know. Besides, if he didn't turn his life over to His healing touch, Mike was going to lose the love of the person he cared for most.

For Ana, the next week passed as if Mike had never worked in the E.R. Not seeing him made her feel as if he'd never existed, never been a part of her life, as if he'd never caressed her cheek or touched her hair, as if he'd never kissed her.

She heard Williams tell Mitchelson that Mike enjoyed working in pedes and was getting plenty of overtime. Other than that, nothing. She didn't see him. No one else mentioned him and she refused to ask questions.

The next Sunday, as Ana got off her shift, she decided to go to church again. She liked the people there, felt a presence like the one Mike had talked about, but she couldn't name. He'd said it was the Holy Spirit. To her, this presence was a feeling of peace and joy, love and healing and something else she couldn't identify, like her soul being touched and changed.

Three hours later, she again slid in next to Brandon. As the associate minister read the scripture halfway through the service, she heard a deep inhalation of breath and saw Francie lean over and gasp. After a few seconds, Francie grabbed her husband's hand and pulled herself to her feet. She whispered to him, "My water broke."

Ana took one of her arms and Brandon the other to support Francie from the sanctuary. Once outside and heading toward the car, Ana said, "How long have you been having contractions?"

"They started this morning."

"This morning?" Brandon said. "Why didn't you tell me?"

"They weren't hard. I thought they were like those false ones I had last month."

Ana opened the car door and helped Francie inside. "How far apart?"

"Oh, five or ten minutes."

"Brandon, you have plenty of time to get her to the hospital, but get going."

Francie reached out the window and took Ana's arm. "I'd really like you to come with us if you don't mind. I'd feel much better with a doctor in the car."

"Sure." As an E.R. physician, she'd delivered babies. Well, one baby. She always called the obstetrical resident, but Francie didn't need to know that now. Ana got in the backseat in time to see the rest of the family running from the church.

"Meet you at the hospital," Brandon shouted and drove off.

After a few hours in the waiting room, Mike was a wreck. Brandon remained in the birthing room and brought frequent reports. Ana had disappeared, but Manny turned up to wait with Julie. They all paced.

Mike went to work in pedes at three but asked Tim to bring him reports. Doing something, keeping busy should make the time go faster, but it didn't. Mike glanced at his watch every few minutes, but it seemed as if the hands never moved. At five, Tim silently dashed through the third floor hall to tell Mike the baby was on the way. After checking out with the head nurse, Mike ran upstairs after his brother.

When they were finally allowed to see Francie and Brandon an hour later, the baby had been whisked off to the nursery.

"What's his name?" Tim held Francie's hand.

"He's Michael Timothy Fairchild," Francie said. "Named for my favorite cousins because you two really are my brothers."

Tim laughed and Mike grinned more widely than he had for days. Mike grabbed his brother's arm and pulled him toward the door. "Come on. We're going to the nursery to see our baby." He waved at the new parents as they left.

Once there, they stood outside the large window and searched the infant's face to see who he looked like. "I think he has your big ears," Tim said.

While Mike tried to think of an insult, he heard someone approach from behind him.

"He's a beautiful baby," Ana said.

"Yeah." Mike guessed he had a huge smile, which became even wider when he saw her. Filled with joy about the baby and from seeing Ana, he took her hand, but she pulled it quickly away. He deserved that.

"Did you know Francie named him for Mike and me?" Tim asked.

"That's terrific." She turned to walk away.

"Ana," Mike said, but she didn't pause. Silently he watched her walk away, furious with himself. What a mess he'd made. Was there any way he could explain to her how messed up he'd felt?

Could he make things right between them again? He had to. He could learn little by little what trust and love meant. Could love heal the break between them?

At seven-fifteen Tuesday morning, Mike waited outside the E.R. for Ana. When she saw him, she said, "Goodbye, Fuller," and headed toward the parking lot.

He deserved that, too. So wrapped up in his misery, so egocentric in his pain, he had treated her as if she weren't important, as if he couldn't trust her. Now, he'd have to paddle really fast to win her back.

He followed her. "Ana, could I talk to you? Please."

She turned toward him. "Why?" she said, only that. Interest didn't show in her eyes nor eagerness in her stance.

"I made a mistake. I need to apologize."

"Oh." She waved her hand toward him. "Don't worry about it." She headed away from him. "I'm fine."

He sprinted behind her and caught up at the edge of the parking lot. "Please. I want to talk to you."

She rolled her eyes. "Mike, you said you're too busy to bother with me."

"I didn't mean it that way."

"Well, that's the way it came out. I don't want to go through this off-and-on stuff. I don't want a relationship with a guy who retreats when the going gets rough because he doesn't care enough to share."

"It's not that I don't care." He took her hand and led her toward the low brick wall that separated the hospital and the lot. "I don't communicate well. I'm sorry. I must have hurt you." He gently tugged on her hand so she'd sit down next to him.

"I'm not going to lie. You did hurt me, but that may be good. The pain made me realize that the man I want to be with is a lot like my father. Papi drove my mother crazy with his moods." She stood. "I'm not going to live that way no matter how much I care about you. I refuse."

"No matter how much you care?" He got to his feet. "Do you still care?"

"Mike, did you hear the part about how I'm not

going to put up with the great stone face, no matter how handsome and charming and smart you are, no matter how much I care? I refuse to do that."

"Please come back. Please talk to me." He motioned toward the wall. "I heard you, I did. Now, at this moment, I *want* to talk. I want to communicate."

With reluctant steps, Ana returned to the wall and sat down.

When he realized it was all up to him, that Ana wasn't going to make this easy, Mike cleared his throat. "Okay, this is why I pulled away from you. Here's what happened. I'm sharing." She didn't look impressed. "I'm worried about Tim. I found him sneaking out of the house the night I went home sick."

"Isn't he eighteen?"

"Yes, but I've told you about my family. We don't make good decisions. I don't believe Tim can handle being out all night with the group of guys he hangs with. He knew this wasn't a good idea or he wouldn't have climbed out the window."

She nodded.

"He was supposed to go see the recruiting officer a couple of times, but he never showed up for the appointments. Now I don't know what he's going to do. Plus, with our being sick and Mom taking care of us, there's no money coming in but a lot going out." He shook his head before he dropped it in his hands. "I was exhausted from being sick for a long time. I couldn't handle it all. I did what I've always done. I shut everyone out. I shut you out."

Ana sat still for a moment. He watched her face and searched her expression, trying to figure out how she felt, but found nothing. She studied the crepe myrtle, pink and white against the wall of the hospital, while the breeze moved the curling tendrils of her hair.

"Why didn't you talk to me about your problems?"

"I'm a guy."

She sighed. "I believe there may be a few men someplace who communicate. I'm not asking all that much, but you could have mentioned you were having problems and that you'd decided to transfer to pediatrics."

Yeah, he should have.

"Why are you so frightened?" she asked.

There was a moment of silence. Then she looked at him, squarely in the eyes and said, "Do you think if I knew how tough your life is, I'd reject you like Cynthia did?"

He couldn't answer. He felt as if he'd been

punched in the stomach, hard, and his breath had been knocked out. Did he really feel that way? "I hadn't thought about it like that." He paused to consider her question, amazed he hadn't recognized what had been so easy for Ana to see. "I guess I did, deep inside."

She stood again. He wished she'd stop doing that. "You have to learn to trust me," she said. "I'm not Cynthia. I'm not at all like Cynthia."

"I know that. I trust you."

"Mike, you don't know anything about trust, and you wouldn't recognize love if it bit you in the leg."

"Do you love me?" He moved around in front of her and took her hand.

"I love a lot about you, but that doesn't change a thing." She pulled her hand away. "I refuse to be in love by myself."

"Ana, please give me another chance."

Gazing up at him, she said, "Mike, I don't trust you."

At least she called him Mike this time, but the part about not trusting him scared him.

"I'm different now."

"You're feeling good because of the baby, but when hard times come again, you'll close me out. I know that. If you love someone, you have to share the good times and the bad, but you won't allow me to be with you and to support you. I can't commit my life to you if you're not able to share your life with me, every bit of your life."

"I don't know how to do that." The confession hurt to make. "I wish I did."

"I know you had a tough childhood and that you're going through hard times." She turned her head away from him. "I can't go through this today-I'm-happy-but-tomorrow-who-knows? stuff with you. It tears me apart." She looked back to study him. "I need to know you're with me for the long term. I need to know if you want that kind of relationship."

"Ana, you have to accept the fact I can't share as much as you want."

She considered his words. "Okay, I can live with that, but I need you to *try* to share, especially the difficult moments. I won't settle for less. Do you love me? Are you willing to make the effort?"

He wanted to tell her how much he needed and loved her but the words wouldn't come. He nodded.

"You can't say it." She took a step toward her car. "When you can promise to share with me, when you can say the words, I'll listen, but I warn you. I'm not going to wait forever."

With the words stuck in his throat, he watched her walk away, unable to stop her. Pain filled him.

Then he remembered the scripture.

"Okay, Lord," he said. "It's You and me together. What I have to do is really difficult, and I need You to share the burden." As the words left his mouth, he felt relieved, as if a load had been lifted from him. He had no idea what to do next, but he wasn't alone.

As she drove out of the parking lot, Ana felt like speeding down the road and shouting at the other drivers to get out of the way. Oh, she didn't, of course, but she *felt* like it. Yes, she was in a real mood because she'd done it again. She'd been Miss I'm-Always-Right, demanding that everything be done *her* way.

She was used to being in control. She was comfortable with that. Being in charge was how she ran her life—but Mike kept her off balance. With him, she wasn't in charge, which completely frustrated her. She had no idea how to handle loss of power and hadn't coped very well today. Yes, she'd blown it. He'd tried but she hadn't.

When she realized she was close to the diner, she slowed and pulled into a parking place by the little park. She should not be driving while she felt this way. Pushing the car door open, she got out, closed it and wandered down the path. Instead of sitting on a bench, she ambled around the rose-bushes before kneeling down to yank a weed out here and there.

With each one she jerked out, her stress decreased. Finally, she stood, picked up the bunch of leaves, stems and roots and tossed them in the trash. She smoothed the mulch before surveying the area. It looked better.

Calmer now, she wiped her hands on a tissue and threw it in the barrel on top of the weeds. Then she settled on a bench and stared herself in the face, metaphorically. She did not like what she saw.

In the past few days, she'd attempted to fill the hole Mike's absence had left with work and with prayer. Work was easy. In the hospital, everyone hurried, dashed from place to place and had almost every minute filled with motion. But there were times in the E.R. when she'd look around for Mike, expecting him to be moving a gurney or transporting a patient or assisting her, and he wasn't there.

When she tried to sleep, she imagined the whisper of Mike's finger across her cheek. She wished she could taste the sweetness of his lips against hers. She longed to see his rare smile or run her fingers through his shaggy hair, to rub her hand along the rough shadow of his whiskers.

Every thought brought bittersweet tears, but she blinked them back. She never cried. Never—until she met Mike. Tough and determined, she'd always forced herself through every obstacle, climbed all the barriers that had blocked her way, fought every problem.

But not this one. She couldn't force herself to forget Mike Fuller. What a wimp she was to yearn for a man who didn't trust her.

Another worry overshadowed that one. Even if Mike wanted to see her again, she wasn't sure they could make it. And the problem wasn't Mike. It was her. She didn't know how to change, how to give up her need to control.

Her father had told her yesterday that he'd proposed to Mike's mother and felt sure she'd say yes. He'd looked so happy. In fact, he and Tessie always looked delighted just to be together. They didn't fight. They helped each other, understood each other. Tessie did little things for her dad, fixed him special dishes, made cute little drawings. Her father basked in the attention and returned it in the way of small gifts and hugs.

She was so happy for him and for Tessie, too, but their joy made her wonder. Maybe she wasn't meant to be part of a couple. Maybe she was too demanding, too sure of herself and her decisions to allow another person into her life.

As she started toward the car, Ana remembered the scripture from the other Sunday and prayed, "Dear Lord, help me to share Mike's burdens, to be more loving and accepting. Lead me to turn control of my life over to You."

But the thought of actually doing that terrified her, filling her with a strange aimless feeling. In that state, she didn't know what to do next, about Mike, about herself, or their lives.

Chapter Sixteen

❧

"Antonio and I are getting married."

As her words penetrated the information he was reading on diabetes, Mike looked up at his mother and Mr. Ramírez standing in the middle of the living room. He dropped the book and jumped to his feet. "Great." He hugged his mother then reached out to shake Mr. Ramírez's hand. "Congratulations. I'm happy for you."

He moved over to sit in a folding chair and waved for the couple to sit on the sofa. "Tell me about it. When did he propose?"

"Antonio proposed last week, but I asked him to give me a few days to think about it. You know—" she smiled at her fiancé then at Mike "—my first marriage didn't work out too well."

"But Mr. Ramírez isn't at all like my father."

"No, he isn't. Antonio is wonderful." Her eyes shone with happiness. "We haven't set a date yet."

He studied Ana's father. He hated it, but Mike had to ask, "Sir, do you mind having me for a stepson? After all, I did hurt your daughter."

"Well, it didn't make me happy, but these are your lives, yours and Ana's. You two have to work it out," Mr. Ramírez said. "I learned a long time ago not to meddle in Ana's business."

Mike felt like a father checking out a young man's intentions toward his daughter, but he had to ask the next question, too. "How do you feel about Mom's background, about her record?"

"At first, it was hard to accept." The older man nodded. "But I love your mother. What she did, she did for you boys, and she's never going to break the law again."

Mike watched Mr. Ramírez, who beamed at Mom. Ana had called her father "Mr. Stone-face," just as she had Mike, but Mr. Ramírez didn't look that way. Love had changed one Mr. Stone-face. Could it do the same for Mike, or was he too afraid to try?

"I'd like to get married next month." Mr. Ramírez dragged his eyes from his mother. "We're getting older every day, and I want to share every minute I can with my Tessie."

"Oh, Antonio." She slapped his arm like a girl with her first crush before she said, "I want to make sure everything is fine with the boys first."

"Mom." Mike leaned forward. "Your boys are both adults. You don't have to worry about us anymore."

"But Tim still acts so young."

"If you wait until Tim grows up, you may never get married."

"I thought that army stint was all set up, but the recruiter called this morning," she said. "It seems Tim never kept his appointments."

"Don't worry about Tim. I'll talk to him, try to get that straightened out." He took his mother's hand, the one Mr. Ramírez wasn't holding. "Don't worry about us. Concentrate on the wedding and how happy you're going to be."

Mike paused, then turned to Mr. Ramírez. "Do you mind if I talk to my mother for a few minutes?"

"Not at all. I'll wait outside." Mr. Ramírez kissed his mother's cheek then left the house.

"Are you sure you want to get married?" Mike moved to sit next to his mother on the sofa. "Don't hurry into this because you think it will make my life easier."

"Oh, yes, I'm sure. I love him." She glanced

toward the window where she could see Mr. Ramírez standing outside. "He takes care of me."

Mike could see his mother was ecstatic. He really hadn't needed to ask, but there was still something more he needed to know. "But this is so soon. You haven't known him long."

"Sometimes love comes fast."

"Are you sure you want to get married in a month?"

"Darling—" she turned, her gaze capturing Mike's "—when one reaches a certain age, everything in the body begins to go." She whispered the next words. "I want to get married while I can still hold it all together."

His mouth dropped open. He couldn't answer. She tugged her hand from his and spun toward the door in a swirl of her brilliant green skirt.

When she waved and closed the door behind her, he fell onto the sofa and had the best laugh he'd enjoyed in weeks.

For the conversation with Tim, Mike tried to bribe his brother into a good mood with pizza. Before his older brother could say a word, Tim said, "I talked to my recruiting officer today." Then he took a black olive from Mike's side and paused to pop it in his mouth. "I'm going to start basic in three weeks."

"Three weeks?" Mike almost choked on the bite he'd taken. "I thought basic started in two months."

"The recruiter and I decided there was no reason for delay. I'd rather get basic over than keep working at the burger place."

"Makes sense."

Imagine that. Tim made sense.

Both of these events simplified Mike's life greatly. With his mother and brother settled, he could concentrate on his future. What about going back to medical school? And could those plans include Ana, or had he acted like too much of a jerk and lost her?

If he wanted a future with Ana—but there really was no question about that—he wanted to spend the rest of his life with her. He'd have to work hard to win her back. His last effort hadn't been dazzlingly successful, but now he knew what Ana wanted. She'd raised the bar, but this time he'd fight for her. He was determined to get her back.

After a few days, no plan of action had come to mind. He'd considered several alternatives and had wisely decided against kidnapping. A romantic picnic wouldn't work because she wouldn't go with him. Her absence would cut down a great deal on the romance and efficacy. Another thought was a quirky date that would impress her but that wouldn't work, either, for the same reason the picnic wouldn't.

Although he wasn't sure that was true. He'd seen her yesterday in the hall, and she hadn't run. Did that mean anything? Maybe so, which made the last alternative seem possibly successful.

That last alternative was waylaying her. He hadn't ruled this idea out yet but wasn't sure of the details.

Except for a quick glance of her in the hall of the hospital every once in a while, he'd left Ana alone for a few days in the hope she'd mellow. That hadn't happened. At least, he hadn't noticed any sign of obvious thawing like a hug or a huge smile or, well, anything other than a friendly expression. He was looking for a lot more than friendly.

Now he had come up with an idea, a more aggressive strategy.

During his break that evening, he went to the chapel to pray. Although no plan to patch things up with Ana came to mind, he decided this was the place he'd bring her to apologize, to share, to show trust, to say everything and anything Ana needed to know. Here, where God had listened to him and helped him find his way, he'd present his case before God and Ana.

So waylaying Ana and taking her to the chapel became the plan. As sketchy as it was, this was the best, as well as the only inspiration he had. He figured the rest was up to Jesus.

The next morning after shift change, he leaned against the hood of Ana's car and waited for her in the parking lot outside the E.R. The only way she could get away was to run over him. He didn't think her anger had reached that level.

When she showed up, her eyes widened and her lips curled into a smile, but that faded quickly. Oddly, she didn't look angry, but what was that emotion? Disappointment? Guilt? Unhappiness? He couldn't tell because she turned away so fast.

"Hey, Fuller." She jingled her keys. "Need a ride?"

"No, thanks." He walked around the side of the car. "I'd like to talk to you."

She glanced up at him, her keys still jingling as if she were nervous, too. "Mike, I'm very confused right now. I'm trying to make sense of our, um, situation. I don't know how to react, what to say."

"I do." He put his arm on the top of the car and gazed down at her. "I love you."

She blinked a couple of times as he tried to decipher her expression. Did her reaction mean anything? Maybe not. Maybe she had a lash caught in her eye. She didn't move away, but she didn't say anything, either.

"See, I can say the words. I love you."

"Mike," she said in a voice husky with pain and deep emotion. "I've wanted to hear those words, but first I need to talk to you, to figure out what's happening. I haven't worked things out in my mind yet. I don't want either of us to hurt anymore, and I'm afraid that's going to happen."

"Why do you assume I'll hurt you?" He took her hand. "I love you. Do you still love me?"

A long pause followed his question while she considered it. Then she dropped her eyes to the ground. "Yes," she whispered and tried to tug her hand away. "But that doesn't mean everything's going to be terrific. Sometimes love isn't enough. Sometimes people are too different."

"I've changed. At least, I'm trying. I know what you need. You said I need to share every bit of my life with you. I'm ready to do that."

When she didn't answer but stopped pulling on her hand, he said, "Please, come with me so we can talk privately."

Still hesitant and unconvinced, she bit her lip. "Mike, I've been wrong. I have to tell you that first." She walked toward the wall and tugged him behind her. Once they sat, he watched her silently.

"Mike, some of what I said before was true. I can't be in love by myself and you have to trust me enough to share."

"I'm working on that."

"The problem is that you *did* share. You confessed to me that you don't know how to share, and I didn't do anything to help you."

He kept his gaze on her face and tried to comprehend her words. She was apologizing for not helping him? That was an idea he'd never considered. "Ana—"

She held up her hand. "No, this is my confession, and I'm not very good at this sort of thing." With a deep breath, she said, "Did I help you at all? No, I lectured you and walked off. I didn't listen to you or offer to share your burdens. I didn't even *push* you to communicate."

He stretched out his arm and placed it around her. She didn't pull away but leaned closer to him.

"Mike, I walked away from you." Her voice quivered. "On top of that, I acted so superior, as if *I* don't have any faults."

"None that I can see." He smiled.

"Oh, sure." She bit her lip. "How 'bout starting that list with my total lack of compassion and going on from there?"

"Ana, you're being really hard on yourself."

"It's about time. When am I going to learn to accept people, both their faults and strengths? When will I understand that, no matter how determined I am, I can't change other people. Most people are just fine and perfectly happy as they are."

"Maybe they're not. Maybe they're waiting for you to rescue them, to head them in the right direction."

"Right." She rolled her eyes. "Mike, I don't know how to give up control any more than you know how to communicate."

"Okay, we can work on all that. Will you give us a chance to tackle the problems together?"

At her uncertain nod, he got to his feet and pulled her up after him. "Now, it's my turn. Come with me? I need to tell you something, too."

"Why can't you tell me here?" She looked back at the wall.

"Because I'd like to tell you in the chapel. I want to talk to you in His presence."

"That would mean a lot to you," she said, still cautious.

"Wouldn't it mean a lot to you, too?"

Ana shoved the keys back in her purse and allowed him to lead her toward the hospital. With his arm still on her shoulder, she remembered his

words. He loved her. He'd said that. Mike
wouldn't tell her he loved her if he didn't mean
it. If she considered herself tough and determined,
why didn't she have the courage to try again?

As they turned a corner into an empty hall, she
looked at Mike and smiled. He grinned back at
her and pulled her closer to him. She knew he
wanted to kiss her, but this was neither the appro-
priate place or the right time. They still had a lot
to work through.

When they arrived at the chapel, Mike opened
one of the wide doors for her. She stepped inside
and heard the loud vroom of the vacuum. Other
members of the housecleaning crew dusted the
pews and straightened the Communion table. The
scent of lemon polish and dust permeated the air.

Mike watched in disappointment before he
smiled. "Sometimes plans don't come together,"
he said. "I thought this would be perfect, but I
know another place."

Taking her hand again, he headed toward the
bank of elevators. "We should have privacy there."

They got off on the third floor and walked down
the hall. Mike stopped before a door. The sign
affixed to it said Linen closet 312A.

"Why did you stop?" She studied Mike who
was looking back and forth down the corridor.

Then he opened the door, shoved her inside and closed it behind them.

"This is the place."

"This is the place?" She turned around. Shelves covered with piles of sheets and towels surrounded them.

"Well, with the chapel busy, I thought of this, the only other private place in the hospital." He followed her scrutiny of the tiny area. "It's private and, after all, God is everywhere, as much with us here as in the chapel."

"Well, yes, but…" She stopped talking when she saw how serious he had become. "Won't we be interrupted?" she asked.

"No, they don't start changing beds for an hour."

The forty-watt bulb in the fixture on the high ceiling didn't emit much light, but it showed Mike's face. She yearned to reach out and smooth away his worried expression but this wasn't the time. Not yet.

"I told you about my family, what's going on with them and about how worried I've been," he began.

She nodded.

"That's why…" Mike started to say.

At exactly that moment, a redheaded man pulled the door open and stood there staring. Ana didn't know the orderly's name, but Mike turned toward him and said, "Hey, Hugo, give us a few minutes, okay?"

"Okay, but we're going to need more towels pretty soon." Hugo grabbed a stack and shut the door.

"Okay, one more time," Mike turned back toward her. "I've shared a lot with you, although most of it was because you pulled it out of me."

"Well, I…" she began in an effort to explain herself.

"I'm glad you did. I don't know how to share. We didn't communicate well in my family or in any of the others where I lived. It was always easier to keep everything inside. That way, no one would laugh at me or use what I said to get me back later or make me feel guilty because I'd made my mother worry. I learned to keep everything in. It's habit by now."

She didn't know what to say. The thought of Mike as a little boy being afraid to communicate hurt.

"But you don't let me get away with that," he said. "That's one reason I love you."

"Because I'm a pushy woman?" She cringed.

He nodded. "I need that. You have to understand I'll never share with you as completely as you want me to. I don't open up easily, but I'll try." He looked at her as if he'd asked a question.

"Okay," she said, although she still wondered what was next. "I can accept that. Go on."

He began looking around, his eyes darting from the bulb to the floor, caressing her face quickly before moving his gaze to the shelves of linen.

"What's wrong? Why are you so nervous?" She placed her hand on his shoulder.

"I'm going to tell you something I've only told one person before. It's hard for me to talk about." He swallowed. "Almost impossible. I didn't tell Cynthia this, but I have to share it with you. I want you to know how much I love you and trust you."

When he didn't say more, Ana rubbed her thumb against his lips. "Go ahead. I'm listening."

He opened and closed his mouth several times without a word emerging. Finally, he whispered, "When I was eighteen, I knocked over a convenience store."

That was all he said. One sentence, and it rocked her. Mike Fuller had committed a robbery?

"What?" she gasped and dropped her hand. "You did what?"

He turned away, just a little, so he didn't have to see her face. Probably preferred not to see the horror written there.

Recognizing his pain was greater than hers, she took his chin and gently turned his face toward her. "Go ahead."

"Okay." He stared at the towels on a shelf

behind her. "When I was eighteen, Francie took me to the store to buy a loaf of bread. For some reason—I don't know what. I didn't know then and I don't know now. Just plain stupidity." He stopped and took another deep breath. "I told you we Fullers don't make good decisions, that we feel the call to the wild side." He paused. "Anyway, I robbed it."

When he didn't speak for almost a minute, she said, "Go on."

"After my cousin let me out of the car, I pulled on a ski mask and walked inside. The cashier saw me, pulled a wad of cash from the register and gave it to me, handed it right over to me." He looked at his hands as if he could still see the money there. "I grabbed it, ran out of the store and got into the car." He stopped and rubbed his hand across his eyes.

"What happened next?" She attempted to keep her voice calm because Mike's trembled and broke.

"That's the worst part, the part I really hate to talk about." He dropped his head and, she thought, whispered a prayer before he started the story again. "When I got to the car, Francie knew what I'd done. I mean, I had money coming out of the pocket of my jacket and held a ski mask. In Texas, there's only one reason anyone has a ski mask, and it isn't to keep your face warm."

"What did she say?"

"Nothing. She drove around the corner, took the money, face mask and jacket and shoved me out of the car. Then she went to the cops, showed them everything, and confessed to the robbery."

Ana gasped. "What?"

"I didn't know until weeks later that she'd taken the fall for me. She was in prison by the time I found out, and I couldn't do a thing about it."

"Did you talk to her?"

He nodded. "When I found out she was locked up, I visited her and told her I was going to confess. She said it wouldn't do any good because they already had her for the job. All she wanted was for me to become a doctor. A prison record would destroy that." He dragged his hand through his hair. "I think it was more her dream than mine at the time. I can never repay her enough for what she did for me. I'm really ashamed about this. The robbery was stupid." He dropped his face into his hands. "It wasn't a big thrill. It cost Francie a good chunk of her life for nothing. For nothing."

Ana didn't know how to react. This man she loved wasn't the person she'd thought. He'd robbed a store and allowed his cousin to go to prison for it. Her effort at acceptance had taken a sharp turn and become harder than she'd imagined.

"Did you ever try to take responsibility?"

He lifted his face. "When Francie and Brandon were dating, I told him. He said there was nothing I could do about it. The case was so unimportant, they'd never retry it. Besides, everyone would believe Francie. She's very convincing." After a deep breath, he continued, "I still feel guilty. Francie and Brandon have forgiven me, but I don't know if I can forgive myself."

She didn't say a word. She couldn't. She was shaken and stunned. None of the thoughts tumbling through her brain fit the situation.

"You wanted me to share, so you'd know I trust you," Mike said. "I don't know what more I can say. Now you know the worst thing I've ever done. I've changed. I believe the years since have made me a better person. Ana, this is who I am, the man my life has made me. Can you accept me?"

"I need to think." She held on to a shelf and lowered herself to the floor. "It's not easy. I wasn't expecting this. It's hard for me to grasp and even harder to understand."

He kneeled beside her. "I know how difficult this must be for you to take in. Because I love you, because I'm working so hard to change, I hope you still love me and can forgive me."

"I can't pretend this doesn't shake me, Mike."

She clasped her hands in front of her. "You're a different person than I thought, a man with a criminal background. I have to think about this."

He didn't say a word, didn't contradict her or try to explain.

And yet, he'd attempted to take the blame for the robbery twice; he'd left medical school to care for his mother and brother, even when it meant losing his fiancée. He'd worked hard as an orderly and was determined to become a doctor. Children loved him, and children always recognized a fraud.

And he'd turned his life over to God.

Could she forgive him for that crime and for allowing Francie to take the fall? But Francie had chosen to go to jail because she loved her cousin.

She glanced into his face and saw such pain, so much suffering and hurt. How could she say she was trying to become a Christian and not forgive a man who looked and sounded so penitent? Who had changed so much? No matter how hard this was for her, the guilt and despair were killing Mike.

"Have you prayed about this?" she asked.

"Over and over. I believe God has forgiven me."

"You said Francie has."

"She was furious I did such a stupid thing, but she forgave me. That's who Francie is. That's why we all love her so much."

Ana remembered her uncle who'd gone to prison. Those years had been hard on his family, but they'd accepted the prodigal back. Wasn't that the whole point of the parable? Of the gospel?

Oh, Lord, lead me. I don't know what to do, but You can guide me. She sat in the silence and listened. In only a few seconds, peace and compassion filled her. Reaching her hand out, she allowed Mike to help her stand.

"Mike, your past is hard for me to accept, even harder for me to understand, but that was six years ago." She searched for the right words. "Since then, you've changed. You've become a fine young man, a person anyone would be proud to know."

"Ana, can *you* accept me?"

"I've seen people change. I know it's possible." She stopped her words. Mike had asked her to trust him. What she was about to say would be irrevocable. She paused to order her thoughts and speak carefully as he continued to study her.

"First, I believe that if Francie and God have forgiven you, you have to forgive yourself."

He nodded and continued to scrutinize her face, so nervous his hand shook a little as he grasped hers. "And you? Can you accept me?"

"I'm trying. Give me a little time, I'm really trying."

He didn't say anything but took her other hand. His eyes scanned her expression as if he were searching for clues. "You know where I've been. You know who I am."

She nodded, still too filled with emotion to say more. What was it her father had said about Tessie? Something about seeing the person she was becoming. Could she do the same with Mike?

He pulled her toward him. "I don't have much to offer, but I can promise you this. I will love you forever."

She allowed almost a minute to pass as she considered and prayed, remembering the robbery had been years ago. Suddenly it was easy. She loved him. Her mind cleared and the words tumbled from her mouth. "You're everything I could ever want in a man, Mike. I love you." When she said that, she felt free, filled with happiness and the conviction this was the right decision.

He put his arms around her and leaned his cheek against her hair. "Thank God," he whispered. "Thank You, God." Then he lifted his face and gazed into her eyes. "I love you, Ana. I'll try to show that in everything I do." He smiled, that wonderful smile that warmed her. "Don't even think of changing. I need you to keep after me, because if you don't, I might go back to the old, silent Mike. Your determination is one of the things I love about you."

"You love me because I'm pushy?" she asked again.

"Well, not always, but most of the time. Sometimes it drives me crazy."

"Then you must really love me to put up with that."

"Yeah, I do. Without your encouragement, I won't know that you love me."

"Oh, you'll know." She put her head against his chest and basked in the knowledge that they were together and sharing, both of them. "You'll always know that."

"It's too soon to ask you to marry me, but I will. I want to be with you for the rest of my life." He held her, his embrace showing her the depth of his love.

Outside, she could hear the chime of the elevators, the sound of people passing and their worried voices, the echo of footsteps getting closer. She figured the latter probably belonged to Hugo who wanted to get his towels.

But here, inside this most ordinary of places, she felt the presence of the spirit. She heard the beat of Mike's heart and felt his loving touch. This was everything she needed.

As she heard the doorknob turn, Ana allowed joy to fill her. In Mike's arms, in a linen closet at Austin University Hospital with the aroma of disinfectants tickling her nose was exactly where she wanted to be.

Epilogue

Mike looked down the pew. On the other end, Francie sat next to Brandon, who held their two-month-old son. As Mike watched, Francie put her hand on her husband's and smiled into his eyes.

Next to Brandon were Tessie and Antonio, the newlyweds. Closer to him were Julie, Quique and Raúl. Of course, Ana sat next to Mike. On her finger she wore a ring with a tiny diamond, the only one he could afford. Ana loved it. When she placed her hand on Mike's arm, he smiled down at her. *Thank You, God, for bringing me this woman who loves me enough to break down my barriers.*

On Mike's left, Tim looked handsome with his short military buzz. One more thing to be thankful for. Tim was growing up and becoming more responsible although Mike doubted if he'd ever be conventional. His own man—that was who Tim was.

Sitting with him on that pew were the greatest gifts anyone could ever receive, his family in Christ. They were all here because a few years earlier, her feet hurting and tired after a long day of work, Francie had entered a church and allowed God to transform her.

Life was truly like a pond, its ripples reaching out to touch others. When she'd entered a church and found faith, God hadn't stopped with Francie. That experience had touched and brought this group together. As crowded as they were into this pew, soon they were going to expand to another as family brought more family and witnessed to their friends.

They were truly blessed.

Grabill Missionary Church Library
P.O. Box 279
13637 State Street
Grabill, IN 46741

Dear Reader,

One of my favorite hymns is "Take It to the Lord in Prayer." It reminds me we can share our burden with the Lord. When life was rough, Mike Fuller learned to accept the healing touch of his Savior, as well as the love of Ana Ramírez.

Trying to go it alone is one of my problems. I imagine many of us share that tendency because we've been taught to be strong, to do everything ourselves. As I wrote this book, I was reminded again that we aren't alone, that we find rest with the one who takes our burden upon Him.

You may remember Mike from THE PATH TO LOVE. He's a member of a family with an unfortunate bent toward crime, but a family that has found faith and has changed. In this book, Mike falls in love with Ana, a doctor from a warm and loving Hispanic family.

Ana and Mike's struggles were difficult, but they triumphed through faith. I pray that this victory will inspire and touch each of you.

Jane Myers Perrine

QUESTIONS FOR DISCUSSION

1. Mike's life was a series of wrong decisions, twists and turns. Ana carefully plotted out her life in a straight line leading to where she was determined to go. Which is more like you? As you look back, how did your choices—bad, as well as good—lead you to where you are now? What part did God play on this journey?

2. Mike is lost and doesn't have any idea what to do next. Have you ever felt this way? If so, what did you do?

3. Ana is certain that she can do everything she wants if she works hard enough. Is this realistic? Does Ana change? Can she accept the idea that sometimes there are barriers and that failure is not always a disaster? Can we accept and use failure for good?

4. Ana tells Mike that because Francie has forgiven him and God has forgiven him, he should forgive himself. Do you believe people often hold on to guilt and shame even after they repent? Are there people who find it difficult to forgive themselves? What problems might this cause?

5. Mike discovers something he's always known: Jesus is always with us to share our burdens. When has this been important in your life? Have you seen a willingness to shoulder the load alone in the lives of friends or family members? What often happens when we attempt to carry the burdens ourselves? Why are people so determined to be strong when there are others who can share our problems and troubles?

6. Mr. Ramírez says he loves Tessie for the person she is becoming. Who are you becoming? Are there people you love for the people they are becoming?

7. Have you hidden a dark secret from a person you care about or has someone hidden a secret from you? Did this action hurt your relationship? How? Do you believe there may be secrets we don't need to share with the people we love? Why or why not?

8. What did you think about Ana's reaction to Mike's revelation? How would you have reacted?

9. Ana finally recognizes that her determination to succeed has made her judgmental and con-

trolling. Do you believe she can let go of these traits? Do you know people like this? How can they change? Do they need to change? Why? Can faith help? How?

10. When you're going through tough times, what scripture helps you? Many find the Twenty-third Psalm helpful. Do you? Have you found strength in the verses from Matthew that spoke to both Mike and Ana?

HEARTWARMING INSPIRATIONAL ROMANCE

Contemporary,
inspirational romances
with Christian characters
facing the challenges
of life and love
in today's world.

**NOW AVAILABLE IN REGULAR
AND LARGER-PRINT FORMATS.**

**Steeple
Hill®**

For exciting stories that reflect traditional values,
visit:
www.SteepleHill.com

LIGEN07R

Love Inspired®
SUSPENSE
RIVETING INSPIRATIONAL ROMANCE

Watch for our new series of
edge-of-your-seat suspense novels.
These contemporary tales
of intrigue and romance
feature Christian characters
facing challenges to their faith...
and their lives!

**Steeple
Hill®**

Visit:
www.SteepleHill.com

LISUSDIR07R